Washington Irving

Westminster Abbey and Christmas Sketches

Washington Irving

Westminster Abbey and Christmas Sketches

ISBN/EAN: 9783743387317

Manufactured in Europe, USA, Canada, Australia, Japa

Cover: Foto ©Andreas Hilbeck / pixelio.de

Manufactured and distributed by brebook publishing software
(www.brebook.com)

Washington Irving

Westminster Abbey and Christmas Sketches

ENGLISH CLASSIC SERIES.—No. 93.

WESTMINSTER ABBEY

AND

CHRISTMAS SKETCHES.

WESTMINSTER ABBEY.	CHRISTMAS DAY.
CHRISTMAS EVE.	THE CHRISTMAS DINNER.

BY

WASHINGTON IRVING.

𝔚𝔦𝔱𝔥 𝔑𝔫𝔱𝔯𝔬𝔡𝔲𝔠𝔱𝔬𝔯𝔶 𝔞𝔫𝔡 𝔈𝔵𝔭𝔩𝔞𝔫𝔞𝔱𝔬𝔯𝔶 𝔑𝔬𝔱𝔢𝔰.

NEW YORK:

EFFINGHAM MAYNARD & CO., PUBLISHERS,

771 BROADWAY AND 67 & 69 NINTH STREET.

A Complete Course in the Study of English.

Spelling, Language, Grammar, Composition, Literature.

REED'S WORD LESSONS—A COMPLETE SPELLER.
REED'S INTRODUCTORY LANGUAGE WORK.
REED & KELLOGG'S GRADED LESSONS IN ENGLISH.
REED & KELLOGG'S HIGHER LESSONS IN ENGLISH.
REED & KELLOGG'S ONE-BOOK COURSE IN ENGLISH.
KELLOGG'S TEXT-BOOK ON RHETORIC.
KELLOGG'S TEXT-BOOK ON ENGLISH LITERATURE.

In the preparation of this series the authors have had one object clearly in view—to so develop the study of the English language as to present a complete, progressive course, from the Spelling-Book to the study of English Literature. The troublesome contradictions which arise in using books arranged by different authors on these subjects, and which require much time for explanation in the school-room, will be avoided by the use of the above "Complete Course."

Teachers are earnestly invited to examine these books.

Effingham Maynard & Co., Publishers,

771 Broadway, New York.

LIFE OF IRVING.

Washington Irving, one of the earliest and most popular of American authors, and of whom Thackeray happily spoke as "the first ambassador whom the New World of Letters sent to the Old," was born in New York City, in 1783. He received only a common-school education, leaving the school-room at sixteen, yet for many years afterward pursued a systematic course of reading of the standard authors, especially Chaucer, Spenser, and Bunyan. In his boyhood days he seemed to have a natural talent for writing essays and stories. As he always detested mathematics, he often wrote compositions for his school-mates, and they in turn worked out his problems for him. He studied law for a time, but not being inclined to submit to the drudgery of a profession, preferred to employ himself in rambling excursions around Manhattan Island, by which he became familiar with the beautiful scenery which he afterward made famous by his pen. Thus he acquired that minute knowledge of various historical locations, curious traditions, and legends, so beautifully made use of in his *Sketch-Book* and *History of New York*. In 1804, being threatened with pulmonary disease, he sailed for Europe, and remained abroad for nearly two years. On his return, he undertook to resume his legal practice, but without success. In company with others, he began the publication of a serial called "Salmagundi." It was well conducted, and proved successful. In 1809, he published his *Knickerbocker's History of New York*, "the most unique, perfectly rounded, and elaborately sustained burlesque in our literature." He conducted a magazine in Philadelphia for two years, to which he contributed articles afterward included in the *Sketch-Book*. In 1814, he served as an aid to Governor Tompkins, and at the end of the war again went to Europe, where he continued to live for the next seventeen years. By the failure of his brother, he lost all his property, and having been thus thrown upon his own resources, he devoted himself to literature to earn a living. His *Sketch-Book* was published in 1819. By the personal influence of Sir Walter Scott it was republished in London, and at once established Irving's reputation as a great author.

3

His next works were *Bracebridge Hall*, published in 1822, and *Tales of a Traveler*, in 1824. Having been commissioned to make some translations from the Spanish, he took up his residence in Madrid. To this residence in Spain we are indebted for some of his most charming works, as, *Life of Columbus, Conquest of Granada, The Alhambra, Mahomet and his Successors*, and *Spanish Papers*. He returned to America in 1832. During the next ten years were published *Astoria, Adventures of Captain Bonneville*, and *Wolfert's Roost*. In 1842, Irving was appointed Minister to Spain. His *Life of Goldsmith* was published four years later, after his return home. His last and most carefully written work was the *Life of Washington*, in five volumes.

Irving's last years were passed at "Sunnyside," his delightful residence at Tarrytown, on the Hudson, in the midst of the beautiful scenes which he has immortalized. Irving died Nov. 28, 1859, the same year with Prescott, the historian, and Macaulay. A friend who saw much of our author in his latter days thus describes him: "He had dark gray eyes, a handsome straight nose, which might perhaps be called large; a broad, high, full forehead, and a small mouth. I should call him of medium height, about five feet and nine inches, and inclined to be a trifle stout. His smile was exceedingly genial, lightening up his whole face, and rendering it very attractive; while if he were about to say any thing humorous, it would beam forth from his eyes even before his words were spoken."

In one of his charming "Easy Chair" essays, George William Curtis says:—"Irving was as quaint a figure as the Diedrich Knickerbocker in the preliminary advertisement of the *History of New York*. Thirty years ago he might have been seen on an autumnal afternoon, tripping with an elastic step along Broadway, with low quartered shoes neatly tied, and a Talma cloak—a short garment like the cape of a coat. There was a chirping, cheery, old school air in his appearance which was undeniably Dutch, and most harmonious with the association of his writing. He seemed, indeed, to have stepped out of his own books; and the cordial grace and humor of his address, if he stopped for a passing chat, were delightfully characteristic. He was then our most famous man of letters, but he was simply free from all self-consciousness and assumption and dogmatism."

WASHINGTON IRVING. 1783—1859.

"Washington Irving! Why, gentlemen, I don't go upstairs to bed two nights out of the seven without taking Washington Irving under my arm."—*Charles Dickens.*

"I know of no books which are oftener lent than those that bear the pseudonym of 'Geoffrey Crayon.' Few, very few, can show a long succession so pure, so graceful, and so varied, as Mr. Irving."—*Mary Russell Mitford.*

"Rich and original humor, great refinement of feeling and delicacy of sentiment. Style accurately finished, easy, and transparent. Accurate observer : his descriptions are correct, animated, and beautiful."—*George S. Hillard.*

"If he wishes to study a style which possesses the characteristic beauties of Addison's, its ease, simplicity, and elegance, with greater accuracy, point, and spirit, let him give his days and nights to the volumes of Irving."—*Edward Everett's Advice to a Student.*

"He seems to have been born with a rare sense of literary proportion and form ; into this, as into a mold, were run his apparently lazy and really acute observations of life. That he thoroughly mastered such literature as he fancied there is abundant evidence ; that his style was influenced by the purest English models is also apparent. But there remains a large margin for wonder how, with his want of training, he could have elaborated a style which is distinctly his own, and is as copious, felicitous in the choice of words, flowing, spontaneous, flexible, engaging, clear, and as little wearisome when read continuously in quantity as any in the English tongue."—*C. D. Warner.*

"In his family, gentle, generous, good-humored, affectionate, self-denying ; in society, a delightful example of complete gentlemanhood ; quite unspoiled by prosperity ; never obsequious to the great ; eager to acknowledge every contemporary's merit ; always kind and affable with the young members of his calling : in his professional bargains and mercantile dealings delicately honest and grateful. He was, at the same time, one of the most charming masters of our lighter language ; the constant friend to us and our nation ; to men of letters doubly dear, not for his wit and genius merely, but as an exemplar of goodness, probity, and a pure life."—*Wm. M. Thackeray.*

REFERENCES.

For full particulars concerning Irving's personal and literary career, the student is referred to Curtis's *Homes of American Authors*, Duyckinck's *American Literature*, Tuckerman's Sketch, and Bryant's Oration, delivered a few years ago, and since republished in a volume of essays. Read also the Life of Irving in Hill's series of *Great American Authors*, and an essay by Charles D. Warner, originally printed in the *Atlantic*, for March, 1880, and since revised and published as the first volume of *American Men of Letters*, a series of biographies of eminent American authors.

Studies of Irving is a little book containing the essays by Warner and Bryant, and *Personal Reminiscences*, by George P. Putnam. An exhaustive biography of Irving has been written by his nephew, Pierre Irving.

PRINCIPAL WRITINGS.

Sketch-Book; History of New York; Bracebridge Hall; Tales of a Traveler; Life of Columbus; Conquest of Granada; Alhambra; Tour of the Prairies; Abbotsford and Newstead Abbey; Astoria; Adventures of Captain Bonneville; Life of Goldsmith; Life of Washington.

SELECTIONS TO READ.

The student is advised to begin with the *Sketch-Book*. The following are some of the best sketches:

1. The Wife. 2. Rip Van Winkle. 3. Rural Life in England. 4. The Broken Heart. 5. The Widow and her Son. 6. The Mutability of Literature. 7. Westminster Abbey. 8. Christmas. 9. Christmas Eve. 10. Christmas Day. 11. The Christmas Dinner. 12. The Pride of the Village. 13. The Legend of Sleepy Hollow.

After the *Sketch-Book*, the whole or certain chapters of the *Life of Goldsmith* may be read, especially in connection with the study of Goldsmith's text. Sketches similar to those in the *Sketch-Book* may be found in *Bracebridge Hall, Traveler, Crayon Miscellany*, and other volumes. Certain chapters in *Knickerbocker's History of New York* will be found very interesting.

INTRODUCTION.

WESTMINSTER ABBEY, as the coronation church of the sovereigns of England from the time of Harold, and on account of its proximity to the seat of English government, has acquired a fame and importance which in a certain sense outvie those of St. Paul's. It occupies the site of a chapel built by Siebert, in honor of St. Peter, on a slightly elevated spot of London rising from the marshy ground bordering the Thames. A church of greater pretensions was erected by King Edward about 980 ; but, this church being partly demolished by the Danes, Edward the Confessor founded within the precincts of his palace an abbey and church in the Norman style of architecture, which was completed in 1065, and of which there now only remain the pyx house to the south of the abbey, the substructure of the dormitory, and the south side of the cloisters. The rebuilding of the church was commenced in 1220 by Henry III., who erected the choir and transepts, and also a lady chapel, which was removed to make way for the chapel of Henry VII. The building was practically completed by Edward I., but the greater part of the nave in the Transition style of architecture, and various other improvements, were added down to the time of Henry VII., including the west end of the nave, the deanery. portions of the cloisters, and the Jerusalem chamber ; while the two towers at the west end were erected by that famous architect, Sir Christopher Wren, who had no proper appreciation of Gothic architecture. The length of the church, including Henry VII.'s chapel, is 531 feet, or, excluding it, 416 feet ; the breadth of the transepts, 203 feet ; the height of the church, 102 feet, and of the towers 225 feet. The choir, where the coronation of English sovereigns takes place, is a fine specimen of Early English, with decorations added in the 14th century, and contains among other tombs those of Siebert, king of the East Saxons, Anne of Cleves, and Edmund Crouchback,

7

earl of Leicester. The north transept is occupied principally with monuments of warriors and statesmen, and, in the south transept, the "poet's corner" contains memorials of most of the great English writers from Chaucer to Thackeray and Dickens. The nave with its clustered columns, its beautiful *triforium*, and its lofty and finely proportioned roof, is the most impressive portion of the interior. The monuments in its north and south aisles are of a very miscellaneous character, and commemorate musicians, men of science, travellers, patriots, and adventurers. The monuments in the chapels of St. Benedict, St. Edmund, St. Nicholas, St. Paul, St. Erasmus, St. John the Baptist, and the Abbot Islip are chiefly to ecclesiastics and members of the nobility. Henry VII.'s chapel, which is remarkable for the fretted vault-work of the roof, with its magical fan tracery, contains beside the monument of Henry VII. the tombs of many English sovereigns and their children, and also of various other personages of historic fame. In the chapel of Edward the Confessor are the shrine of Edward the Confessor, in Purbeck marble, the altar tomb of Edward I., the coronation chair of the English sovereigns, and the stone of Scone, the old coronation seat of the Scottish kings. In the chapter-house (1250) the meetings of the Commons took place before they were transferred to St. Stephen's Chapel; and in the Jerusalem chamber (1376-86), where Edward V. is said to have been born and Henry IV. was brought to die, the sittings of the lower house of convocation of the province of Canterbury are now held.

The Jerusalem Chamber is so called probably from its old tapestries or pictures of the history of Jerusalem. Originally this was but a with-dawing room or guest-chamber of the abbot, opening on one side into the abbot's refectory, and on the other into his garden.

The communion-table in Westminster is the only one in England which has any authoritative claim to the name of "altar."

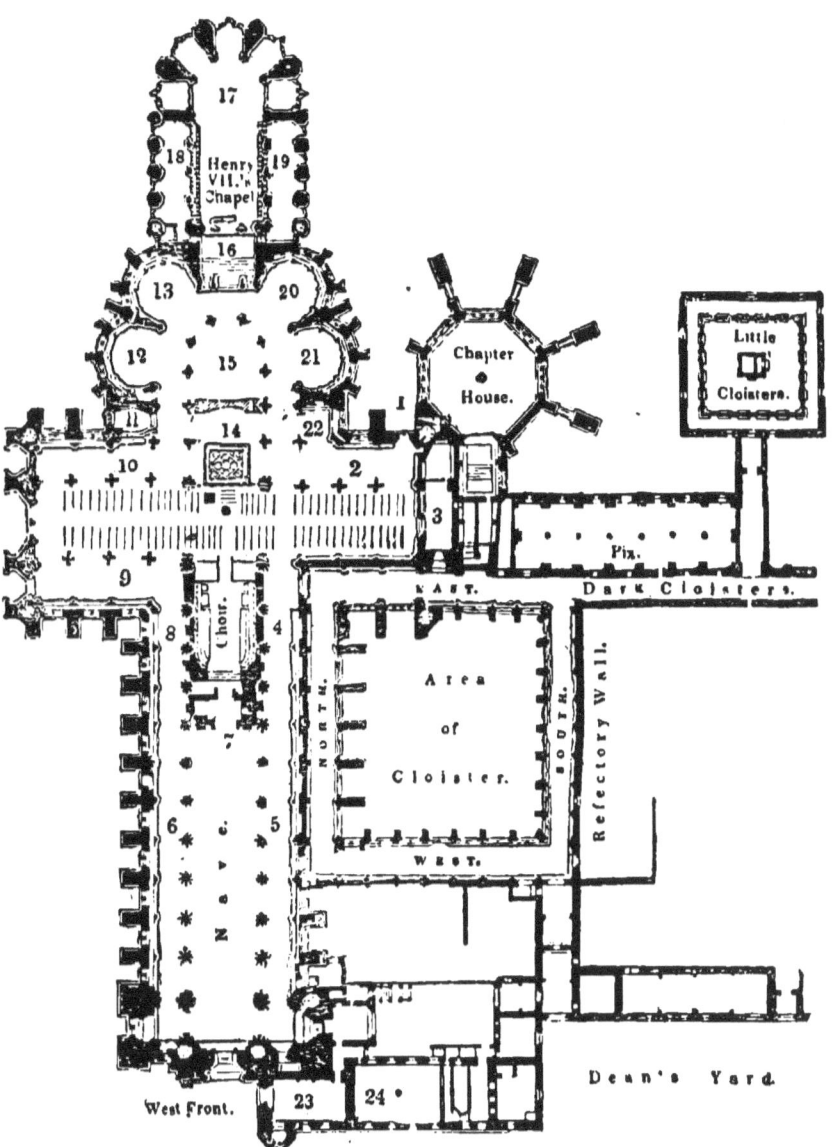

PLAN OF WESTMINSTER ABBEY.

1. General Entrance.
2. Poets' Corner.
3. St. Blaize's Chapel.
4. South Aisle of Choir.
5. South Aisle of Nave.
6. North Aisle of Nave.
7. New Screen.
8. North of Choir.
9. West Aisle of North Transept.
10. East Aisle of North Transept.
11. Islip's Chapel.
12. St. John the Baptist's.
13. St. Paul's.
14. Abbot Ware's Mosaic Pavement.
15. Edward the Confessor's Chapel and Shrine.
16. Porch to Henry VII.'s Chapel.
17. Henry VII.'s Tomb.
18. North Aisle of Henry VII.'s Chapel.
19. South Aisle of Henry VII.'s Chapel.
20. St. Nicholas's Chapel.
21. St. Edmund's.
22. St. Benedict's.
23. Jerusalem Chamber.
24. College (formerly Abbey) Dining-hall.

WESTMINSTER ABBEY.

When I beheld, with deep astonishment,
To famous Westminster how there resorte,
Living in brasse or stony monument,
The princes and the worthies of all sorte;
Doe not I see reformde nobilitie,
Without contempt, or pride, or ostentation,
And looke upon offenseless majesty,
Naked of pomp or earthly domination ?
And how a play-game of a painted stone
Contents the quiet now and silent sprites,
Whome all the world which late they stood upon,
Could not content nor quench their appetites.
    Life is a frost of cold felicitie,
    And death the thaw of all our vanitie.
            Christolero's Epigrams, by T. B., 1598.

On one of those sober and rather melancholy days in the latter part of autumn, when the shadows of morning and evening almost mingle together, and throw a gloom over the decline of the year, I passed several hours in rambling about Westminster Abbey. There was something congenial to the season in the mournful magnificence of the old pile ; and as I passed its threshold, it seemed like stepping back into the regions of antiquity, and losing myself among the shades of former ages.

I entered from the inner court of Westminster school, through a long, low, vaulted passage, that had an almost subterranean look, being dimly lighted in one part by circular perforations in the massive walls. Through this dark avenue, I had a distant view of the cloisters,[1] with the figure of an old verger,[2] in his black gown, moving along their shadowy vaults,

---

1. **The cloisters.**—The cloisters were begun by the Confessor and finished shortly after the Conquest. They were the place of recreation, gossip, intercourse and business for the monastic community.
2. **Verger.**—The official who takes care of the church building.

11

and seeming like a specter from one of the neighboring tombs.

The approach to the abbey through these gloomy monastic remains, prepares the mind for its solemn contemplation. The cloister still retains something of the quiet and seclusion of former days. The gray walls[3] are discolored by damps, and crumbling with age; a coat of hoary moss has gathered over the inscriptions of the mural monuments,[4] and obscured the death's heads,[5] and other funeral emblems. The sharp touches of the chisel are gone from the rich tracery of the arches; the roses which adorned the key-stones[6] have lost their leafy beauty; everything bears marks of the gradual dilapidations of time, which yet has something touching and pleasing in its very decay.

The sun was pouring down a yellow autumnal ray into the square of the cloisters; beaming upon a scanty plot of grass in the center, and lighting up an angle of the vaulted passage with a kind of dusky splendor. From between the arcades, the eye glanced up to a bit of blue sky, or a passing cloud; and beheld the sun-gilt pinnacles of the abbey towering[7] into the azure heaven.

As I paced the cloisters, sometimes contemplating this mingled picture of glory and decay, and sometimes endeavoring to decipher the inscriptions on the tombstones, which formed the pavement beneath my feet, my eyes were attracted to three figures, rudely carved in relief, but nearly worn away by the footsteps of many generations. They were the effigies[8]

---

3. **The gray walls.**—"There is one religious structure in the kingdom that stands in its original finishing, exhibiting all those modest hues that the native appearance of the stone so pleasingly bestows. This structure is the Abbey Church of Westminster. . . . There I find my happiness the most complete. This church has not been *whitewashed.*"—John Carter, *Gent. Mag.*, 1799.

4. **Mural monuments.**—The various memorials about the walls.

5. **Death's heads.**—Naked human skulls personifying death.

6. **Key-stones.**—The key-stone is the topmost stone of an arch.

7. **Towering.**—The spires of Westminster were 225 feet high.

8. **Effigies.**—It was once a feature of the great funerals to have a waxen effigy of the deceased person on a platform highly decorated with black hangings. It remained for a mouth in the abbey, near the grave; but in the case of sovereigns a much longer time. The effigies here referred to are, of course, of stone.

of three of the early abbots;[9] the epitaphs were entirely effaced; the names alone remained, having no doubt been renewed in later times ; (Vitalis. Abbas. 1082, and Gislebertus Crispinus. Abbas. 1114, and Laurentius. Abbas. 1176.) I remained some little while, musing over these casual relics of antiquity, thus left like wrecks upon this distant shore of time, telling no tale but that such beings had been and had perished ; teaching no moral but the futility of that pride which hopes still to exact homage in its ashes, and to live in an inscription. A little longer, and even these faint records will be obliterated, and the monument will cease to be a memorial. Whilst I was yet looking down upon the gravestones, I was roused by the sound of the abbey clock, reverberating from buttress to buttress, and echoing among the cloisters. It is almost startling to hear this warning of departed time sounding among the tombs, and telling the lapse of the hour, which, like a billow, has rolled us onward towards the grave.

HENRY III.
(From his tomb in Westminster Abbey, London.)

I pursued my walk to an arched door opening to the interior of the abbey. On entering here, the magnitude of the building breaks fully upon the mind, contrasted with the vaults of the cloisters. The eye gazes with wonder at clustered columns of gigantic dimensions, with arches springing from them to such an amazing height ; and man wandering about their bases, shrunk into insignificance in comparison with his own handi-work. The spaciousness and gloom of this vast edifice

9. **Three of the early abbots.**—Irving really mentions four: Vitalis, Gislebert, Crispin, and Laurence. These were Norman abbots. In Vitalis's time the first history of the abbey was written by one of the monks Sulcard. Laurence procured from the Pope the canonization of the Confessor.

produce a profound and mysterious awe. We step cautiously and softly about, as if fearful of disturbing the hallowed silence of the tomb; while every footfall whispers along the walls, and chatters among the sepulchres, making us more sensible of the quiet we have interrupted.

It seems as if the awful nature of the place presses down upon the soul, and hushes the beholder into noiseless reverence. We feel that we are surrounded by the congregated bones of the great men of past times, who have filled history with their deeds, and the earth with their renown. And yet it almost provokes a smile at the vanity of human ambition, to see how they are crowded together, and jostled in the dust; what parsimony is observed in doling out a scanty nook—a gloomy corner—a little portion of earth, to those whom, when alive, kingdoms could not satisfy: and how many shapes, and forms, and artifices, are devised to catch the casual notice of the passenger, and save from forgetfulness, for a few short years, a name which once aspired to occupy ages of the world's thought and admiration.

I passed some time in Poet's Corner,[10] which occupies an end of one of the transepts or cross aisles of the abbey. The monuments are generally simple; for the lives of literary men afford no striking themes for a sculptor. Shakespeare[11] and

---

10. **Poet's corner.**—This is the name applied to the Southern transept. It derived its origin from the death of Chaucer who died while Clerk of the Royal Works in the palaces of Westminster and Windsor. He was appointed by Richard II., and although he held the office but twenty months it evidently gave him a place in the royal household that was not forgotten at his death.

11. **Shakespeare** died April 23, 1616, and was buried at Stratford.

> Renowned Spenser, lie a thought more nigh
> To learned Chaucer: and rare Beaumont lie
> A little nearer Spenser, to make room
> For Shakespeare in your three-fold four-fold tomb.

To this Ben Jonson replies :

> My Shakespeare rise, I will not lodge thee by
> Chaucer or Spenser, or bid Beaumont lie
> A little farther off to make thee room.
> Thou art a monument without a tomb,
> And art alive still while thy book doth live,
> And we have wits to read, and praise to give.

The attempt was never made to "move his bones," nor was his monument erected till 1740.

Addison [12] have statues erected to their memories; but the greater part have busts, medallions, and sometimes mere inscriptions. Notwithstanding the simplicity of these memorials, I have always observed that the visitors to the abbey remain longest about them. A kinder and fonder feeling takes place of that cold curiosity or vague admiration with which they gaze on the splendid monuments of the great and the heroic. They linger about these as about the tombs of friends and companions; for indeed there is something of companionship between the author and the reader. Other men are known to posterity only through the medium of history, which is continually growing faint and obscure; but the intercourse between the author and his fellow-men is ever new, active, and immediate. He has lived for them more than for himself; he has sacrificed surrounding enjoyments, and shut himself up from the delights of social life, that he might the more intimately commune with distant minds and distant ages. Well may the world cherish his renown; for it has been purchased, not by deeds of violence and blood, but by the diligent dispensation of pleasure. Well may posterity be grateful to his memory; for he has left it an inheritance, not of empty names and sounding actions, but whole treasures of wisdom, bright gems of thought, and golden veins of language.

From Poet's Corner I continued my stroll towards that part of the abbey which contains the sepulchres [13] of the kings, I wandered among what once were chapels, but which are now occupied by the tombs and monuments of the great. At every turn, I met with some illustrious name, or the cognizance of some powerful house renowned in history. As the eye darts into these dusky chambers of death, it catches

---

12. **Addison.**—Joseph Addison died June 17, 1719. His body lay in state in the Jerusalem chamber, and was borne thence to the abbey at dead of night. The choir sang a funeral hymn, and Bishop Atterbury met the corpse and led the procession by torch-light to the chapel of Henry VII. It was not till 1808 that a memorial was erected. It represents Addison clad in his dressing-gown and freed from his wig, stepping from his parlor at Chelsea into his trim little garden with his work for the next day's *Spectator* just finished.
13. **Sepulchre of the kings.**—See illustration.

glimpses of quaint effigies : some kneeling [14] in niches, as if in devotion; others stretched upon the tombs, with hands piously pressed together; warriors in armor, as if reposing after battle; prelates, with crosiers and mitres; and nobles in robes and coronets, lying as it were in state. In glancing over this scene, so strangely populous, yet where every form is so still and silent, it seems almost as if we were treading a mansion of that fabled city where every being had been suddenly transmuted into stone.

RICHARD II.
(Jerusalem Chamber, Westminster Abbey.)

I paused to contemplate a tomb on which lay the effigy of a knight in complete armor.

A large buckler was on one arm ; the hands were pressed together in supplication upon the breast; the face was almost covered by the morion ; the legs were crossed in token of the warrior's having been engaged in the holy war. It was the tomb of a crusader; of one of those military enthusiasts, who so strangely mingled religion and romance, and whose exploits form the connecting link between fact and fiction—between the history and the fairy tale. There is something extremely picturesque in the tombs of these adventurers, decorated as they are with rude armorial bearings and Gothic sculpture. They comport with the antiquated chapels in which they are generally found; and

14. Some kneeling. See illustration, p. 17.

In considering them, the imagination is apt to kindle with the legendary associations, the romantic fictions, the chivalrous pomp and pageantry, which poetry has spread over the wars for the Sepulchre of Christ.[15] They are the relics of times utterly gone by; of beings passed from recollection; of customs and manners with which ours have no affinity. They are like objects from some strange and distant land of which we have no certain knowledge, and about which all our conceptions are vague and visionary. There is something extremely solemn and awful in those effigies on Gothic tombs, extended as if in the sleep of death, or in the supplication of the dying hour. They have an effect infinitely more impressive on my feelings than the fanciful attitudes, the over-wrought conceits, and allegorical groups, which abound on modern monuments. I have been struck, also, with the superiority of many of the old sepulchral inscriptions. There was a noble way, in former times, of saying things simply, and yet saying them proudly : and I do not know an epitaph that breathes a loftier consciousness of family worth and honorable lineage, than one which affirms, of a noble house, that "all the brothers were brave, and all the sisters virtuous."

EDWARD III.
(From portrait, Painted Chamber, Westminster.)

In the opposite transept to Poet's Corner, stands a monu-

---

15. **Wars for the sepulchre of Christ.**—The crusades. From an early period in the history of the church it was considered a pious act to make a pilgrimage to the Holy Sepulchre, and to visit the spots consecrated by the presence of the Saviour, but it was not until about the end of the 11th century that an organized expedition, known as the first of the seven crusades, started for the Holy Land.

ment which is among the most renowned achievements[16] of modern art; but which, to me, appears horrible rather than sublime. It is the tomb of Mrs. Nightingale,[17] by Roubillac. The bottom of the monument is represented as throwing open its marble doors, and a sheeted skeleton is starting forth. The shroud is falling from his fleshless frame as he launches his dart at his victim. She is sinking into her affrighted husband's arms, who strives, with vain and frantic effort, to avert the blow. The whole is executed with terrible truth and spirit; we almost fancy we hear the gibbering yell of triumph, bursting from the distended jaws of the spectre.—But why should we thus seek to clothe death with unnecessary terrors, and to spread horrors round the tomb of those we love? The grave should be surrounded by every thing that might inspire tenderness and veneration for the dead; or that might win the living to virtue. It is the place, not of disgust and dismay, but of sorrow and meditation.

While wandering about these gloomy vaults and silent aisles, studying the records of the dead, the sound of busy existence from without occasionally reaches the ear :—the rumbling of the passing equipage; the murmur of the multitude; or perhaps the light laugh of pleasure. The contrast is striking with the deathlike repose around; and it has a strange effect upon the feelings, thus to hear the surges of active life hurrying along and beating against the very walls of the sepulchre.

I continued in this way to move from tomb to tomb, and from chapel to chapel. The day was gradually wearing away; the distant tread of loiterers about the abbey grew less and less frequent; the sweet-tongued bell was summoning to even-

---

16. **Renowned achievements.**—It was when working on the figure of Death in this famous structure that Roubillac one day at dinner suddenly dropped his knife and fork on his plate, fell back in his chair, and then darted forwards and threw his features into the strongest possible expression of fear. A tradition of the abbey records that a robber, coming into the abbey by moonlight, was so startled by the same figure as to have fled in dismay.

17. **Mrs. Nightingale.**—This is known as one of the "monuments of mourners." It was raised in 1734 by her son, to commemorate the premature death of Lady Elizabeth Shirley, wife of Joseph Gascoigne Nightingale.

ing prayers ; and I saw at a distance the choristers, in their white surplices, crossing the aisle and entering the choir. I stood before the entrance to Henry the Seventh's chapel.[18] A flight of steps leads up to it, through a deep and gloomy, but magnificent arch. Great gates of brass, richly and delicately wrought, turn heavily upon their hinges, as if proudly reluctant to admit the feet of common mortals into this most gorgeous of sepulchres.

On entering, the eye is astonished by the pomp of architecture, and the elaborate beauty of sculptured detail. The very walls are wrought into universal ornament, encrusted with tracery, and scooped into niches, crowded with the statues of saints and martyrs. Stone seems, by the cunning labor of the chisel, to have been robbed of its weight and density, suspended aloft, as if by magic, and the fretted roof achieved with the wonderful minuteness and airy security of a cobweb.

Along the sides of the chapel are the lofty stalls of the Knights of the Bath,[19] richly carved of oak, though with the grotesque decorations of Gothic architecture. On the pinnacles of the stalls are affixed the helmets and crests of the knights, with their scarfs and swords ; and above them are

---

18 **Henry the Seventh's chapel.**—Henry VII. determined to found at Westminster a chapel more magnificent than that he had designed at Windsor, a greater than the Confessor's shrine, "in order," according to his will. "right shortly to translate into the same the body and reliques of his uncle of blissful memory, King Henry VI.," but the chapel became the chapel not of Henry VI. but of Henry VII. It is the most signal contrast between his closeness in life and "his magnificence in the structures he hath left to posterity." His pride in its grandeur was commemorated by the ship, vast for those times, which he built, "of equal cost with his chapel, which afterwards, in the reign of Mary, sank in the sea and vanished in a moment.

19. **Knights of the Bath.**—In the reign of George I. a permanent change was effected in one of the accompaniments of the coronation :— namely, the Knights of the Bath. In the earlier coronations it had been the practice of the sovereigns to create a number of knights before they started on their procession from the tower. These knights, being made in time of peace, were not enrolled in any existing order, and for a long time had no special desi nation ; but, inasmuch as one of the foremost, striking and characteristic parts of their admission was the complete attention of their persons on the vigil of their knighthood, as an emblem of the cleanliness and purity of their future profession, they were called Knights of the Bath. The king himself bathed with them. They were completely undressed, placed in large baths and then wrapped in soft blankets. The distinctive name first appears in the time of Henry V.

suspended their banners, emblazoned with armorial bearings, and contrasting the splendor of gold and purple and crimson, with the cold gray fretwork of the roof.   In the midst of this grand mausoleum stands the sepulchre of its founder,—his effigy, with that of his queen, extended on a sumptuous tomb, and the whole surrounded by a superbly wrought brazen railing.

There is a sad dreariness in this magnificence ; this strange mixture of tombs and trophies ; these emblems of living and aspiring ambition, close beside mementos which show the dust and oblivion in which all must sooner or later terminate. Nothing impresses the mind with a deeper feeling of loneliness, than to tread the silent and deserted scene of former throng and pageant.   On looking round on the vacant stalls on the knights and their esquires, and on the rows of dusty but gorgeous banners that were once borne before them, my imagination conjured up the scene when this hall was bright with the valor and beauty of the land ; glittering with the splendor of jewelled rank and military array ; alive with the tread of many feet, and the hum of an admiring multitude. All had passsd away ; the silence of death had settled again upon the place ; interrupted only by the casual chirping of birds, which had found their way into the chapel, and built their nests among its friezes and pendants—sure signs of solitariness and desertion.   When I read the names inscribed on the banners, they were those of men scattered far and wide about the world ; some tossing upon distant seas ; some under arms in distant lands ; some mingling in the busy intrigues of courts and cabinets ; all seeking to deserve one more distinction in this mansion of shadowy honors—the melancholy reward of a monument.

Two small aisles on each side of this chapel present a touching instance of the equality of the grave, which brings down the oppressor to a level with the oppressed, and mingles the dust of the bitterest enemies together.   In one is the sepulchre of the haughty Elizabeth ;[20] in the other is that of

20. **Haughty Elizabeth.**—Queen Elizabeth died March 24, and was bur-

her victim, the lovely and unfortunate Mary.[21] Not an hour in the day, but some ejaculation of pity is uttered over the fate of the latter, mingled with indignation at her oppressor. The walls of Elizabeth's sepulchre continually echo with the sighs of sympathy heaved at the grave of her rival.

A peculiar melancholy reigns over the aisle where Mary lies buried. The light struggles dimly through windows darkened by dust. The greater part of the place is in deep shadow, and the walls are stained and tinted by time and weather. A marble figure of Mary is stretched upon the tomb, round which is an iron railing, much corroded, bearing her national emblem—the thistle. I was weary with wandering, and sat down to rest myself by the monument, revolving in my mind the checkered and disastrous story of poor Mary.

The sound of casual footsteps had ceased from the abbey. I could only hear, now and then, the distant voice of the priest repeating the evening service, and the faint responses of the choir; these paused for a time, and all was hushed. The stillness, the desertion and obscurity that were gradually prevailing around, gave a deeper and more solemn interest to the place :

> For in the silent grave no conversation,
> No joyful tread of friends, no voice of lovers,
> No careful father's counsel—nothing's heard,
> For nothing is, but all oblivion,
> Dust, and an endless darkness.

---

ied April 28, 1603. From Richmond Palace, where she died, the body was brought by the Thames to Westminster :

> The queen did come by water to Whitehall,
> The oars at every stroke did tears let fall.

With these and other like exaggerations, which, however, indicate the excess of the national mourning, she was laid in the abbey. "The city of Westminster was surcharged with multitudes of all sorts of people, in their streets, houses, windows, leads and gutters, that came to see the obsequy; and when they beheld her statue or picture lying upon the head thereof, and a ball and scepter in either hand, there was such a general sighing, groaning, and weeping, as the like has not been seen or known in the memory of man: neither doth any history mention any people, time or state to make like lamentation for the death of their sovereign."—*Stow.*

21. **Mary Queen of Scots** was executed in 1587, and transferred from Peterborough in 1606. The letter is still extant, and now hangs above the site of her grave at Peterborough, in which James I. ordered the removal of her body to the spot where he had commanded a memorial of her to be be made in the Church of Westminster, " in the place where the kings and queens of this realm are commonly interred," that the " like honor might be done to the body of his dearest mother, and the like monument be extant to her, that had been done to his dear sister, the late Queen Elizabeth."

Suddenly the notes of the deep-laboring organ burst upon the ear, falling with doubled and redoubled intensity, and rolling, as it were, huge billows of sound. How well do their volume and grandeur accord with this mighty building! With what pomp do they swell through its vast vaults, and breathe their awful harmony through these caves of death, and make the silent sepulchre vocal!—And now they rise in triumphant acclamation, heaving higher and higher their accordant notes, and piling sound on sound.—And now they pause, and the soft voices of the choir break out into sweet gushes of melody; they soar aloft, and warble along the roof, and seem to play about these lofty vaults like the pure airs of heaven. Again the pealing organ heaves its thrilling thunders, compressing air into music, and rolling it forth upon the soul. What long-drawn cadences! What solemn sweeping concords! It grows more and more dense and, powerful—it fills the vast pile, and seems to jar the very walls—the ear is stunned—the senses are overwhelmed. And now it is winding up in full jubilee—it is rising from the earth to heaven—the very soul seems rapt away, and floated upwards on this swelling tide of harmony!

I sat for some time lost in that kind of reverie which a strain of music is apt sometimes to inspire: the shadows of evening were gradually thickening around me: the monuments began to cast deeper and deeper gloom; and the distant clock again gave token of the slowly waning day.

I arose, and prepared to leave the abbey. As I descended the flight of steps which lead into the body of the building, my eye was caught by the shrine of Edward the Confessor, and I ascended the small staircase that conducts to it, to take from thence a general survey of this wilderness of tombs. The shrine is elevated upon a kind of platform, and close around it are the sepulchres of various kings and queens. From this eminence the eye looks down between pillars and funeral trophies to the chapels and chambers below, crowded with tombs; where warriors, prelates, courtiers, and statesmen, lie mouldering in "their beds of darkness." Close by me stood th great chair of coronation, rudely carved of oak, in the barbarous taste of a remote and Gothic age. The scene seemed almost as if contrived, with theatrical artifice, to produce an effect upon the beholder. Here was a type of the beginning and the end of human pomp and power; here it was literally but a step from the throne to the sepulchre. Would not one think that these incongruous mementos had been gathered together as a lesson to living greatness?—to show it, even in the moment of its proudest exaltation, the neglect and dishonor to which it must soon arrive? how soon that crown which encircles its brow must pass away; and it must lie down in the dust and disgraces of the tomb, and be trampled upon by the feet of the meanest of the multitude? For, strange to tell, even the grave is here no longer a sanctuary. There is a shocking levity in some natures, which leads them to sport with awful and hallowed things; and there are base minds, which delight to revenge on the illustrious dead the abject homage and grovelling servility which they pay to the living. The coffin of Edward the Confessor has been broken open, and his remains despoiled of their funeral ornaments; the scepter has been stolen from the hand of the imperious Elizabeth, and the effigy of Henry the Fifth lies headless. Not a royal monument but bears some proof how false and fugitive is the homage of mankind. Some are plundered, some mutilated; some covered with ribaldry and insult—all more or less outraged and dishonored!

CORONATION CHAIR.
(In Westminster Abbey.)

The last beams of day were now faintly streaming through the painted windows in the high vaults above me; the lower parts of the abbey were already wrapped in the obscurity of twilight. The chapels and aisles grew darker and darker.

The effigies of the kings faded into shadows; the marble figures of the monuments assumed strange shapes in the uncertain light; the evening breeze crept through the aisles like the cold breath of the grave; and even the distant footfall of a verger, traversing the Poet's Corner, had something strange and dreary in its sound. I slowly retraced my morning's walk, and as I passed out at the portal of the cloisters, the door, closing with a jarring noise behind me, filled the whole building with echoes.

EARL OF CHATHAM.
(From his monument, Westminster Abbey.)

I endeavored to form some arrangement in my mind of the objects I had been contemplating, but found they were already falling into indistinctness and confusion. Names, inscriptions, trophies, had all become confounded in my recollection, though I had scarcely taken my foot from off the threshold. What, thought I, is this vast assemblage of sepulchres but a treasury of humiliation; a huge pile of reiterated homilies on the emptiness of renown, and the certainty of oblivion? It is, indeed the empire of Death; his great shadowy palace; where he sits in state, mocking at the relics of human glory, and spreading dust and forgetfulness on the monuments of princes. How idle a boast, after all, is the immortality of a name! Time is ever silently turning over his pages; we are too much engrossed by the story of the present, to think of the characters and anecdotes that give interest to the past; and each age is a volume thrown aside to be speedily forgotten. The idol of to-day pushes the hero of yesterday out of our recollection; and will, in turn, be supplanted by his successor of to-morrow.

" Our fathers," says Sir Thomas Brown, " find their graves in our short memories, and sadly tell us how we may be buried in our survivors." History fades into fable ; fact becomes clouded with doubt and controversy ; the inscription moulders from the tablet ; the statue falls from the pedestal. Columns, arches, pyramids, what are they but heaps of sand—and their epitaphs, but characters written in the dust ? What is the security of a tomb, or the perpetuity of an embalmment ? The remains of Alexander the Great have been scattered to the wind, and his empty sarcophagus is now the mere curiosity of a museum. " The Egyptian mummies, which Cambyses or time hath spared, avarice now consumeth ; Mizraim cures wounds, and Pharoah is sold for balsams." *

What then is to insure this pile, which now towers above me, from sharing the fate of mightier mausoleums ? The time must come when its gilded vaults which now spring so loftily, shall lie in rubbish beneath the feet ; when, instead of the sound of melody and praise, the winds shall whistle through the broken arches, and the owl hoot from the shattered tower —when the garish sunbeam shall break into these gloomy mansions of death ; and the ivy twine round the fallen column ; and the fox-glove hang its blossoms about the nameless urn, as if in mockery of the dead. Thus man passes away ; his name passes from recollection ; his history is a tale that is told, and his very monument becomes a ruin.

---

* Sir Thomas Brown.

CHRISTMAS EVE.

Saint Francis and Saint Benedight
Blesse this house from wicked wight;
From the nightmare and the goblin,
That is hight good fellow Robin;
Keep it from all evil spirits.
Fairies, weazels, rats, and ferrets :
  From curfew-time
  To the next prime.   CARTWRIGHT.

IT was a brilliant moonlight night, but extremely cold ; our chaise whirled rapidly over the frozen ground ; the post-boy smacked his whip incessantly, and a part of the time his horses were on a gallop. "He knows where he is going," said my companion, laughing, "and is eager to arrive in time for some of the merriment and good cheer of the servants hall. My father, you must know, is a bigoted devotee of the old school, and prides himself upon keeping up something of old English hospitality. He is a tolerable specimen of what you will rarely meet with nowadays in its purity,—the old English country gentleman ; for our men of fortune spend so much of their time in town, and fashion is carried so much into the country, that the strong rich peculiarities of ancient rural life are almost polished away. My father, however, from early years, took honest Peacham* for his text-book, instead of Chesterfield ; he determined in his own mind, that there was no condition more truly honorable and enviable than that of a country gentleman on his paternal lands, and, therefore, passes the whole of his time on his estate. He is a strenuous advocate for the revival of the old rural games and holiday observances, and is deeply read in the writers, ancient and modern, who have treated on the subject. Indeed, his favorite range of reading is among the authors who

---

* Peacham's Complete Gentleman, 1622.

flourished at least two centuries since ; who, he insists, wrote and thought more like true Englishmen than any of their successors. He even regrets sometimes that he had not been born a few centuries earlier, when England was itself, and had its peculiar manners and customs. As he lives at some distance from the main road, in rather a lonely part of the country, without any rival gentry near him, he has that most enviable of all blessings to an Englishman, an opportunity of indulging the bent of his own humor without molestation. Being representative of the oldest family in the neighborhood, and a great part of the peasantry being his tenants, he is much looked up to, and, in general, is known simply by the appellation of ' The 'Squire ;' a title which has been accorded to the head of the family since time immemorial. I think it best to give you these hints about my worthy old father, to prepare you for any little eccentricities that might otherwise appear absurd."

We had passed for some time along the wall of a park, and at length the chaise stopped at the gate. It was in a heavy magnificent old style, of iron bars, fancifully wrought at top into flourishes and flowers. The huge square columns that supported the gate were summounted by the family crest. Close adjoining was the porter's lodge, sheltered under dark fir trees, and almost buried in shrubbery.

The post-boy rang a large porter's bell, which resounded through the still frosty air, and was answered by the distant barking of dogs, with which the mansion-house seemed garrisoned. An old woman immediately appeared at the gate. As the moonlight fell strongly upon her, I had a full view of a little primitive dame, dressed very much in antique taste, with a neat kerchief and stomacher, and her silver hair peeping from under a cap of snowy whiteness. She came curtseying forth with many expressions of simple joy at seeing her young master. Her husband, it seemed, was up at the house, keeping Christmas eve in the servants' hall ; they could not do without him, as he was the best hand at a song and story in the household.

My friend proposed that we should alight, and walk through the park to the Hall, which was at no great distance, while the chaise should follow on. Our road wound through a noble avenue of trees, among the naked branches of which the moon glittered as she rolled through the deep vault of a cloudless sky. The lawn beyond was sheeted with a slight covering of snow, which here and there sparkled as the moonbeams caught a frosty crystal : and at a distance might be seen a thin transparent vapor, stealing up from the low grounds, and threatening gradually to shroud the landscape.

My companion looked round him with transport :— " How often," said he, " have I scampered up this avenue, on returning home on school vacations ! How often have I played under these trees when a boy ! I feel a degree of filial reverence for them, as we look up to those who have cherished us in childhood. My father was always scrupulous in exacting our holidays, and having us around him on family festivals. He used to direct and superintend our games with the strictness that some parents do the studies of their children. He was very particular that we should play the old English games according to their original form ; and consulted old books for precedent and authority for every ' merrie disport ;' yet, I assure you, there never was pedantry so delightful. It was the policy of the good old gentleman to make his children feel that home was the happiest place in the world, and I value this delicious home-feeling as one of the choicest gifts a parent could bestow."

We were interrupted by the clamor of a troop of dogs of all sorts and sizes, " mongrel, puppy, whelp and hound, and curs of low degree," that, disturbed by the ringing of the porter's bell and the rattling of the chaise, came bounding open-mouthed across the lawn.

"——The little dogs and all,
Tray, Blanche, and Sweetheart, see, they bark at me ! "

cried Bracebridge, laughing. At the sound of his voice, the bark was changed into a yelp of delight, and in a moment he was surrounded and almost overpowered by the caresses of the faithful animals.

We had now come in full view of the old family mansion, partly thrown in deep shadow, and partly lit up by the cold moonshine. It was an irregular building of some magnitude, and seemed to be of the architecture of different periods. One wing was evidently very ancient, with heavy stone-shafted bow windows jutting out and overrun with ivy, from among the foliage of which the small diamond-shaped panes of glass glittered with the moon-beams. The rest of the house was in the French taste of Charles the Second's time, having been repaired and altered, as my friend told me, by one of his ancestors, who returned with that monarch at the Restoration. The grounds about the house were laid out in the old formal manner of artificial flower beds, clipped shrub-beries, raised terraces, and heavy stone ballustrades, orna-mented with urns, a leaden-statue or two, and a jet of water. The old gentleman, I was told, was extremly careful to pre-serve this obsolete finery in all its original state. He admired this fashion in gardening : it had an air of magnificence, was courtly and noble, and befitting good old family style. The boasted imitation of nature and modern gardening had sprung up with modern republican notions, but did not suit a mon-archical government—it smacked of the levelling system. I could not help smiling at this introduction of politics into gardening, though I expressed some apprehension that I should find the old gentleman rather intolerant in his creed. Frank assured me, however, that it was almost the only in-stance in which he had ever heard his father meddle with politics ; and he believed he had got this notion from a mem-ber of Parliament, who once passed a few weeks with him. The 'Squire was glad of any argument to defend his clipped yew trees and formal terraces, which had been occasionally attacked by modern landscape gardeners.

As we approached the house, we heard the sound of music, and now and then a burst of laughter, from one end of the building. This, Bracebridge said, must proceed from the servants' hall, where a great deal of revelry was permitted, and even encouraged, by the 'Squire, throughout the twelve days of Christmas, provided every thing was done conformably to ancient usage. Here were kept up the old games of hoodman blind, shoe the wild mare, hot cockles, steal the white loaf, bob apple, and snap-dragon; the yule clog, and Christmas candle, were regularly burnt, and the mistletoe, with its white berries, hung up, to the imminent peril of all the pretty house-maids.*

So intent were the servants upon their sports, that we had to ring repeatedly before we could make ourselves heard. On our arrival being announced, the 'Squire came out to receive us, accompanied by his two other sons; one a young officer in the army, home on leave of absence; the other an Oxonian, just from the university. The 'Squire was a fine healthy-looking old gentleman, with silver hair curling lightly round an open florid countenance; in which a physiognomist, with the advantage, like myself, of a previous hint or two, might discover a singular mixture of whim and benevolence.

The family meeting was warm and affectionate; as the evening was far advanced, the 'Squire would not permit us to change our traveling dresses, but ushered us at once to the company, which was assembled is a large old-fashioned hall. It was composed of different branches of a numerous family connection, where there were the usual proportions of old uncles and aunts, comfortable married dames, superannuated spinsters, blooming country cousins, half-fledged striplings, and bright-eyed boarding-school hoydens. They were variously occupied; some at a round game of cards; others conversing round the fire-place; at one end of the hall was a group of the young folks, some nearly grown up, others of a more tender and budding age, fully engrossed by a merry game; and a profusion of wooden horses, penny trumpets, and tattered dolls about the floor, showed traces of a troop of

---

* The mistletoe is still hung up in farm-houses and kitchens, at Christmas; and the young men have the privilege of kissing the girls under it, plucking each time a berry from the bush. When the berries are all plucked, the privilege ceases.

little fairy beings, who, having frolicked through a happy day, had been carried off to slumber through a peaceful night.

While the mutual greetings were going on between young Bracebridge and his relatives, I had time to scan the apartment. I have called it a hall, for so it had certainly been in old times, and the 'Squire had evidently endeavored to restore it to something of its primitive state. Over the heavy projecting fire-place was suspended a picture of a warrior in armor, standing by a white horse, and on the opposite wall hung a helmet, buckler and lance. At one end an enormous pair of antlers were inserted in the wall, the branches serving as hooks on which to suspend hats, whips, and spurs ; and in the corners of the apartment were fowling-pieces, fishing-rods, and other sporting implements. The furniture was of the cumbrous workmanship of former days, though some articles of modern convenience had been added and the oaken floor had been carpeted ; so that the whole presented an odd mixture of parlor and hall.

The grate had been removed from the wide overwhelming fire-place, to make way for a fire of wood, in the midst of which was an enormous log, glowing and blazing, and sending forth a vast volume of light and heat ; this I understood was the yule clog, which the 'Squire was particular in having brought in and illumined on a Christmas eve, according to ancient custom.*

---

*The *yule clog* is a great log of wood, sometimes the root of a tree, brought into the house with great ceremony, on Christmas eve, laid in the fire-place, and lighted with the brand of last year's clog. While it lasted, there was great drinking, singing, and telling of tales. Sometimes it was accompanied by Christmas candles ; but in the cottages, the only light was from the ruddy blaze of the great wood fire. The yule clog was to burn all night : if it went out, it was considered a sign of ill luck.

Herrick mentions it in one of his songs :

> Come bring with a noise,
> My merrie, merrie boys,
> The Christmas Log to the firing ;
> While my good dame she
> Bids ye all be free,
> And drink to your hearts desiring.

The yule clog is still burnt in many farm-houses and kitchens in Eng-

It was really delightful to see the old 'Squire, seated in his hereditary elbow-chair, by the hospitable fireside of his ancestors, and looking around him like the sun of a system, beaming warmth, and gladness to every heart. Even the very dog that lay stretched at his feet, as he lazily shifted his position and yawned, would look fondly up in his master's face, wag his tail against the floor, and stretch himself again to sleep, confident of kindness and protection. There is an emanation from the heart in genuine hospitality, which cannot be described, but is immediately felt, and puts the stranger at once at his ease. I had not been seated many minutes by the comfortable hearth of the worthy old cavalier, before I found myself as much at home as if I had been one of the family.

Supper was announced shortly after our arrival. It was served up in a spacious oaken chamber, the panels of which shone with wax, and around which were several family portraits decorated with holly and ivy. Besides the accustomed lights, two great wax tapers, called Christmas candles, wreathed with greens, were placed on a highly polished beaufet among the family plate. The table was abundantly spread with substantial fare ; but the 'Squire made his supper of frumenty, a dish made of wheat cakes boiled in milk with rich spices, being a standing dish in old times for Christmas eve. I was happy to find my old friend, minced pie, in the retinue of the feast ; and finding him to be perfectly orthodox, and that I need not be ashamed of my predilection, I greeted him with all the warmth wherewith we usually greet an old and very genteel acquaintance.

The mirth of the company was greatly promoted by the humors of an eccentric personage whom Mr. Bracebridge always addressed with the quaint appellation of Master

land, particularly in the north, and there are several superstitions connected with it among the peasantry. If a squinting person come to the house while it is burning, or a person barefooted, it is considered an ill omen. The brand remaining from the yule clog is carefully put away to light the next year's Christmas fire.

Simon. He was a tight brisk little man, with the air of an arrant old bachelor. His nose was shaped like the bill of a parrot; his face slightly pitted with the small-pox, with a dry perpetual bloom on it, like a frost-bitten leaf in autumn. He had an eye of great quickness and vivacity, with a drollery and lurking waggery of expression that was irresistible. He was evidently the wit of the family, dealing very much in sly jokes and innuendoes with the ladies, and making infinite merriment by harpings upon old themes; which, unfortunately, my ignorance of the family chronicles did not permit me to enjoy. It seemed to be his great delight, during supper, to keep a young girl next him in a continual agony of stifled laughter, in spite of her awe of the reproving looks of her mother, who sat opposite. Indeed, he was the idol of the younger part of the company, who laughed at everything he said or did, and at every turn of his countenance. I could not wonder at it; for he must have been a miracle of accomplishments in their eyes. He could imitate Punch and Judy; make an old woman of his hand, with the assistance of a burnt cork and pocket-handkerchief; and cut an orange into such a ludicrous caricature, that the young folk were ready to die with laughing.

I was let briefly into his history by Frank Bracebridge. He was an old bachelor, of a small independent income, which, by careful management, was sufficient for all his wants. He revolved through the family system like a vagrant comet in its orbit, sometimes visiting one branch, and sometimes another quite remote, as is often the case with gentlemen of extensive connections and small fortunes in England. He had a chirping, buoyant disposition, always enjoying the present moment; and his frequent change of scene and company prevented his acquiring those rusty, unaccommodating habits, with which old bachelors are so uncharitably charged. He was a complete family chronicle, being versed in the genealogy, history, and intermarriages of the whole house of Bracebridge, which made him a great favorite with the old folks; he was a beau of all the elder ladies and superannuated spinsters, among whom he was habitually considered rather a young fellow, and he was master of the revels among the children ; so that there was not a more popular being in the sphere in which he moved, than Mr. Simon Bracebridge. Of late years, he had resided almost entirely with the 'Squire, to whom he had become a factotum, and whom he particularly delighted by jumping with his humor in respect to old times, and by having a scrap of an old song to suit every occasion. We had presently a specimen of his last-mentioned talent ; for no sooner was supper removed, and spiced wines and other beverages peculiar to the season introduced, than Master Simon was called on for a good old Christmas song. He bethought himself for a moment, and then, with a sparkle of the eye, and a voice that was by no means bad, excepting that it ran occasionally into a falsetto, like the notes of a split reed, he quavered forth a quaint old ditty :

> Now Christmas is come,
> Let us beat up the drum,
> And call all our neighbors together;
> And when they appear,
> Let us make such a cheer,
> As will keep out the wind and the weather, etc.

The supper had disposed every one to gayety, and an old harper was summoned from the servants' hall, where he had been strumming all the evening, and to all appearance comforting himself with some of the 'Squire's home-brewed. He was a kind of hanger-on, I was told, of the establishment, and though ostensibly a resident of the village, was oftener to be found in the 'Squire's kitchen than his own home ; the old gentleman being fond of the sound of " Harp in hall."

The dance, like most dances after supper, was a merry one : some of the older folks joined in it, and the 'Squire himself figured down several couple with a partner with whom he affirmed he had danced at every Christmas for nearly half a century. Master Simon, who seemed to be a kind of connecting link between the old times and the new, and to be withal a little antiquated in the taste of his accomplishments, evidently piqued himself on his dancing, and was endeavoring to gain credit by the heel and toe, rigadoon, and other graces of the ancient school; but he had unluckily assorted himself with a little romping girl from boarding school, who, by her wild vivacity, kept him continually on the stretch, and defeated all his sober attempts at elegance :—such are the ill-sorted matches to which antique gentlemen are unfortunately prone ?

The young Oxonian, on the contrary, had led out one of his maiden aunts, on whom the rogue played a thousand little knaveries with impunity ; he was full of practical jokes, and his delight was to tease his aunts and cousins ; yet, like all madcap youngsters, he was a universal favorite among the women. The most interesting couple in the dance was the young officer, and a ward of the 'Squire's, a beautiful blushing girl of seventeen. From several shy glances which I had noticed in the course of the evening, I suspected there was a little kindness growing up between them ; and, indeed, the young soldier was just the hero to captivate a romantic girl. He was tall, slender, and handsome ; and, like most young British officers of late years, had picked up various small accomplishments on the continent—he could talk French and Italian, draw landscapes, sing very tolerably, dance divinely ; but, above all, he had been wounded at Waterloo ;—what girl of seventeen, well read in poetry and romance, could resist such a mirror of chivalry and perfection ?

The moment the dance was over, he caught up a guitar, and lolling against the old marble fire-place, in an attitude which I am half inclined to suspect was studied, began the little French air of the Troubadour. The 'Squire, however, exclaimed against having anything on Christmas eve but good old English ; upon which the young minstrel, casting up his eye for a moment, as if in an effort of memory, struck into another strain, and with a charming air of gallantry, gave Herrick's " Night Piece to Julia : "

Her eyes the glow-worm lend thee,
The shooting stars attend thee;
     And the elves also,
     Whose little eyes glow
Like the sparks of fire, befriend thee.

No Will-o'-the'-Wisp mislight thee ;
Nor snake or slow-worm bite thee ;
    But on, on thy way,
    Not making a stay,
Since ghost there is none to affright thee

Then let not the dark thee cumber ;
What though the moon does slumber,
    The stars of the night
    Will lend thee their light,
Like tapers clear without number.

Then, Julia, let me woo thee,
Thus, thus to come unto me ;
    And when I shall meet
    Thy silvery feet,
My soul I'll pour into thee.

The song might or might not have been intended in compliment to the fair Julia, for so I found his partner was called ; she, however, was certainly unconscious of any such application ; for she never looked at the singer, but kept her eyes cast upon the floor ; her face was suffused, it is true, with a beautiful blush, and there was a gentle heaving of the bosom, but all that was doubtless caused by the exercise of the dance : indeed, so great was her indifference, that she was amusing herself with plucking to pieces a choice bouquet of hot-house flowers, and by the time the song was concluded the nosegay lay in ruins on the floor.

The party now broke up the night with the kind-hearted old custom of shaking hands. As I passed through the hall on my way to my chamber, the dying embers of the yule clog still sent forth a dusky glow ; and had it not been the season when " no spirit dares stir abroad," I should have been half tempted to steal from my room at midnight, and peep whether the fairies might not be at their revels about the hearth.

My chamber was in the old part of the mansion, the ponderous furniture of which might have been fabricated in the days of the giants. The room was panelled, with cornices of heavy carved work, in which flowers and grotesque faces were strangely intermingled, and a row of black-looking por-

traits stared mournfully at me from the walls.   The bed was
of rich, though faded damask, with a lofty tester, and stood
in a niche opposite a bow-window.   I had scarcely got into
bed when a strain of music seemed to break forth in the air
just below the window : I listened, and found it proceeded
from a band, which I concluded to be the waits from some
neighboring village.   They went round the house, playing
under the windows.   I drew aside the curtains, to hear them
more distinctly.   The moonbeams fell through the upper part
of the casement, partially lighting up the antiquated apartment.   The sounds, as they receded, became soft and aerial,
and seemed to accord with quiet and moonlight.   I listened
and listened--they became more and more tender and remote
and, as they gradually died away, my head sunk upon the
pillow, and I fell asleep.

CHRISTMAS DAY.

Dark and dull night flie hence away,
And give the honor to this day
That sees December turn'd to May.
* * * * * * *
Why does the chilling winter's morne
Smile like a field beset with corn?
Or smell like to a meade new-shorne,
Thus on a sudden?—come and see
The cause, why things thus fragrant be.
HERRICK.

WHEN I woke the next morning, it seemed as if all the events of the preceding evening had been a dream, and nothing but the identity of the ancient chamber convinced me of their reality. While I lay musing on my pillow, I heard the sound of little feet pattering outside of the door, and a whispering consultation. Presently a choir of small voices chanted forth an old Christmas carol, the burden of which was—

Rejoice, our Saviour he was born
On Christmas day in the morning.

I rose softly, slipt on my clothes, opened the door suddenly, and beheld one of the most beautiful little fairy groups that a painter could imagine. It consisted of a boy and two girls, the eldest not more than six, and lovely as seraphs. They were going the rounds of the house, singing at every chamber door, but my sudden appearance frightened them into mute bashfulness. They remained for a moment playing on their lips with their fingers, and now and then stealing a shy glance from under their eyebrows, until, as if by one impulse, they scampered away, and as they turned an angle of the gallery, I heard them laughing in triumph at their escape.

Everything conspired to produce kind and happy feelings, in this stronghold of old-fashioned hospitality. The window of my chamber looked out upon what in summer would have been a beautiful landscape. There was a sloping lawn, a fine stream winding at the foot of it, and a tract of park beyond, with noble clumps of trees, and herds of deer. At a distance was a neat hamlet, with the smoke from the cottage chimneys hanging over it ; and a church, with its dark spire in strong relief against the clear cold sky. The house was surrounded with evergreens according to the English custom, which would have given almost an appearance of summer ; but the morning was extremely frosty ; the light vapor of the preceding evening had been precipitated by the cold, and covered all the trees and every blade of grass with its fine crystallizations. The rays of a bright morning sun had a dazzling effect among the glittering foliage. A robin perched upon the top of a mountain ash, that hung its clusters of red berries just before my window, was basking himself in the sunshine, and piping a few querulous notes ; and a peacock was displaying all the glories of his train, and strutting with the pride and gravity of a Spanish grandee on the terrace-walk below.

I had scarcely dressed myself, when a servant appeared to invite me to family prayers. He showed me the way to a small chapel in the old wing of the house, where I found the principal part of the family already assembled in a kind of gallery, furnished with cushions, hassocks, and large prayer-books ; the servants were seated on benches below. The old gentleman read prayers from a desk in front of the gallery, and Master Simon acted as clerk and made the responses ; and I must do him the justice to say, that he acquitted himself with great gravity and decorum.

The service was followed by a Christmas carol, which Mr. Bracebridge himself had constructed from a poem of his favorite author, Herrick ; and it had been adapted to a church melody by Master Simon. As there were several good voices among the household, the effect was extremely pleasing ; but I was particularly gratified by the exaltation of heart, and sudden sally of grateful feeling, with which the worthy 'Squire delivered one stanza ; his eye glistening, and his voice rambling out of all the bounds of time and tune :

" 'Tis thou that crown'st my glittering hearth
   With guiltless mirth,
And giv'st me Wassaile bowles to drink
   Spic'd to the brink:

Lord, 'tis thy plenty-dropping hand
   That soiles my land
And giv'st me for my bushell sowne,
   Twice ten for one."

I afterward understood that early morning service was read
on every Sunday and saint's day throughout the year, either by
Mr. Bracebridge or some member of the family. It was once
almost universally the case at the seats of the nobility and
gentry of England, and it is much to be regretted that the
custom is falling into neglect ; for the dullest observer must
be sensible of the order and serenity prevalent in those house-
holds, where the occasional exercise of a beautiful form of
worship in the morning gives, as it were, the key-note to every
temper for the day, and attunes every spirit to harmony.

Our breakfast consisted of what the 'Squire denominated
true old English fare.   He indulged in some bitter lamenta-
tions over modern breakfasts of tea and toast, which he cen-
sured as among the causes of modern effeminacy and weak
nerves, and the decline of old English heartiness : and though
he admitted them to his table to suit the palates of his guests,
yet there was a brave display of cold meats, wine, and ale, on
the sideboard.

After breakfast, I walked about the grounds with Frank
Bracebridge and Master Simon, or Mr. Simon, as he was
called by everybody but the 'Squire. We were escorted by
a number of gentlemen-like dogs, that seemed loungers about
the establishment ; from the frisking spaniel to the steady old
stag-hound—the last of which was of a race that had been in
the family time out of mind—they were all obedient to a dog-
whistle which hung to Master Simon's button-hole, and in the
midst of their gambols would glance an eye occasionally upon
a small switch he carried in his hand.

The old mansion had a still more venerable look in the
yellow sunshine than by pale moonlight ; and I could not but

feel the force of the 'Squire's idea, that the formal terraces, heavily moulded balustrades, and clipped yew trees, carried with them an air of proud aristocracy.

There appeared to be an unusual number of peacocks about the place, and I was making some remarks upon what I termed a flock of them that were basking under a sunny wall when I was gently corrected in my phraseology by Master Simon, who told me that according to the most ancient and approved treatise on hunting, I must say a *muster* of peacocks. "In the same way," added he, with a slight air of pedantry, "we saw a flight of doves or swallows, a bevy of quails, a herd of deer, of wrens, or cranes, a skulk of foxes, or a building of rooks." He went on to inform me that, according to Sir Anthony Fitzherbert, we ought to ascribe to this bird "both understanding and glory; for, being praised, he will presently set up his tail, chiefly against the sun, to the intent you may the better behold the beauty thereof. But at the fall of the leaf, when his tail falleth, he will mourn and hide himslf in corners, till his tail come again as it was.

I could not help smiling at this display of small erudition on so whimsical a subject; but I found that the peacocks were birds of some consequence at the Hall; for Frank Bracebridge informed me that they were great favorites with his father, who was extremely careful to keep up the breed, partly because they belonged to chivalry, and were in great request at the stately banquets of the olden time; and partly because they had a pomp and magnificence about them highly becoming an old family mansion. Nothing, he was accustomed to say, had an air of greater state and dignity, than a peacock perched upon on antique stone balustrade.

Master Simon had now to hurry off, having an appointment at the parish church with the village choristers, who were to perform some music of his selection. There was something extremely agreeable in the cheerful flow of animal spirits of the little man; and I confess that I had been somewhat surprised at his apt quotations from authors who certainly were not in the range of every-day reading. I mentioned this last circumstance to Frank Bracebridge, who told me with a smile that Master Simon's whole stock of erudition was confined to some half-a-dozen old authors, which the 'Squire had put into his hands, and which he read over and over, whenever he had a studious fit ; as he sometimes had on a rainy day, or a long winter evening. Sir Anthony Fitzherbert's Book of Husbandry ; Markham's Country Contentment ; the Tretyse of Hunting, by Sir Thomas Cockayne, Knight ; Isaac Walton's Angler, and two or three more such ancient worthies of the pen, were his standard authorities ; and, like all men who know but few books, he looked up to them with a kind of idolatry, and quoted them on all occasions. As to his songs, they were chiefly picked out of old books in the 'Squire's library, and adapted to tunes that were popular among the choice spirits of the last century. His practical application of scraps of literature, however, had caused him to be looked upon as a prodigy of book-knowledge by all the grooms, huntsmen, and small sportsmen of the neighborhood.

While we were talking, we heard the distant toll of the village bell, and I was told that the 'Squire was a little particular in having his household at church on a Christmas morning ; considering it a day of pouring out of thanks and rejoicing ; for, as old Tusser observed,—

"At Christmas be merry, and *thankful withal*
And feast thy good neighbors, the great with the small."

"If you are disposed to go to church," said Frank Bracebridge, "I can promise you a specimen of my cousin Simon's musical achievements. As the church is destitute of an organ, he has formed a band from the village amateurs, and established a musical club for their improvement ; he has also sorted a choir, as he has sorted my father's pack of hounds according to the directions of Jervaise Markham, in his Country Contentments ; for the bass he has sought out all the ' deep, solemn mouths,' and for the tenor the 'loud ringing mouth,' among the country bumpkins ; and for ' sweet mouths,' he has culled with curious taste among the prettiest lasses in the neighborhood ; though these last, he affirms, are the most difficult to keep in tune ; your pretty female singer being exceedingly wayward and capricious, and very liable to accident."

As the morning, though frosty, was remarkably fine and clear, the most of the family walked to the church, which was a very old building of gray stone, and stood near a village, about half a mile from the park gate. Adjoining it was a low snug parsonage, which seemed coeval with the church. The front of it was perfectly matted with a yew tree, that had been trained against its walls, through the dense foliage of which, apertures had been formed to admit light into the small antique lattices. As we passed this sheltered nest, the parson issued forth and preceded us.

I had expected to see a sleek well-conditioned pastor, such as is often found in a snug living in the vicinity of a rich patron's table, but I was disappointed. The parson was a little meagre, black-looking man, with a grizzled wig that was too wide, and stood off from each ear ; so that his head seemed to have shrunk away within it, like a dried filbert in its shell. He wore a rusty coat, with great skirts, and pockets that would have held the church bible and prayer book : and his small legs seemed still smaller, from being planted in large shoes, decorated with enormous buckles.

I was informed by Frank Bracebridge that the parson had been a chum of his father's at Oxford, and had received this living shortly after the latter had come to his estate. He was a complete black-letter hunter, and would scarcely read a work printed in the Roman character. The editions of Caxton and Wynkin de Worde were his delight ; and he was indefatigable in his researches after such old English writers as have fallen into oblivion from their worthlessness. In deference, perhaps, to the notions of Mr. Bracebridge, he had made diligent investigations into the festive rites and holiday customs of former times ; and had been as zealous in the inquiry, as if he had been a boon companion ; but it was merely with that plodding spirit with which men of adust temperament follow up any track of study, merely because it is denominated learning ; indifferent to its intrinsic nature, whether it be the illustration of the wisdom, or of the ribaldry and obscenity of antiquity. He had pored over these old volumes so intensely, that they seemed to have been reflected into his countenance ; which, if the face be indeed an index of the mind, might be compared to a title-page of black-letter.

On reaching the church-porch, we found the parson rebuking the gray-headed sexton for having used mistletoe among the greens with which the church was decorated. It was, he observed, an unholy plant, profane by having been used by the Druids in their mystic ceremonies ; and though it might innocently employed in the festive ornamenting of halls and kitchens, yet it had been deemed by the Fathers of the Church as unhallowed, and totally unfit for sacred purposes. So tenacious was he on this point, that the poor sexton was obliged to strip down a great part of the humble trophies of his taste, before the parson would consent to enter upon the service of the day.

The interior of the church was venerable, but simple ; on the walls were several mural monuments of the Bracebridges, and just beside the altar, was a tomb of ancient workmanship, on which lay the effigy of a warrior in armor, with his legs crossed, a sign of his having been a crusader. I was told it was one of the family who had signalized himself in the Holy Land, and the same whose picture hung over the fire-place in the hall.

During service, Master Simon stood up in the pew, and repeated the responses very audibly ; evincing that kind of ceremonious devotion punctually observed by a gentleman of the old school, and a man of old family connections. I observed, too, that he turned over the leaves of a folio prayer-book with something of a flourish, possibly to show off an enormous seal-ring which enriched one of his fingers, and which had the look of a family relic. But he was evidently most solicitous about the musical part of the service, keeping his eye fixed intently on the choir, and beating time with much gesticulation and emphasis.

The orchestra was in a small gallery, and presented a most

whimsical grouping of heads, piled one above the other, among which I particularly noticed that of the village tailor, a pale fellow with a retreating forehead and chin, who played on the clarionet, and seemed to have blown his face to a point ; and there was another, a short pursy man, stooping and laboring at a bass viol, so as to show nothing but the top of a round bald head like the egg of an ostrich. There were two or three pretty faces among the female singers, to which the keen air of a frosty morning had given a bright rosy tint : but the gentlemen choristers had evidently been chosen, like old Cremona fiddles, more for tone than looks ; and as several had to sing from the same book, there were clusterings of odd physiognomies, not unlike those groups of cherubs we sometimes see on country tombstones.

The usual services of the choir were managed tolerably well, the vocal parts generally lagging a little behind the instrumental, and some loitering fiddler now and then making up for lost time by travelling over a passage with prodigious celerity, and clearing more bars than the keenest fox-hunter, to be in at the death. But the great trial was an anthem that had been prepared and arranged by Master Simon, and on which he had founded great expectation. Unluckily there was a blunder at the very outset—the musicians became flurried ; Master Simon was in a fever ; everything went on lamely and irregularly, until they came to a chorus beginning, " Now let us sing with one accord," which seemed to be a signal for parting company : all became discord and confusion ; each shifted for himself, and got to the end as well, or, rather, as soon as he could ; excepting one old chorister, in a pair of horn spectacles, bestriding and pinching a long sonorous nose; who, happening to stand a little apart, and being wrapped up in his own melody, kept on a quavering course, wriggling his head, ogling his book, and winding all up by a nasal solo of at least three bars' duration.

The parson gave us a most erudite sermon on the rites and ceremonies of Christmas, and the propriety of observing it, not merely as a day of thanksgiving, but of rejoicing; supporting the correctness of his opinions by the earliest usages of the church, and enforcing them by the authorities of Theophilus of Cesarea, St. Cyprian, St. Chrysostom, St. Augustine, and a cloud more of Saints and Fathers, from whom he made copious quotations. I was a little at a loss to perceive the necessity of such a mighty array of forces to maintain a point which no one present seemed inclined to dispute ; but I soon found that the good man had a legion of ideal adversaries to contend with; having, in the course of his researches on the subject of Christmas, got completely embroiled in the sectarian controversies of the Revolution, when the Puritans made such a fierce assault upon the ceremonies of the church, and poor old Christmas was driven out of the land by proclamation of Parliament.* The worthy parson lived but with times past, and knew but little of the present.

Shut up among worm-eaten tomes in the retirement of his antiquated little study, the pages of old times were to him as the gazettes of the day ; while the era of the Revolution was mere modern history. He forgot that nearly two centuries had elapsed since the fiery persecution of poor mince-pie throughout the land ; when plum porridge was denounced as "mere popery," and roast beef as anti-christian; and that Christmas had been brought in again triumphantly with the merry court of King Charles at the Restoration. He kindled into warmth with the ardor of his contest, and the host of imaginary foes with whom he had to combat; he had a stubborn conflict with old Prynne and two or three other forgotten

---

* From the " Flying Eagle," a small Gazette, published December 24th, 1652—"The House spent much time this day about the business of the Navy, for settling the affairs at sea, and before they rose, were presented with a terrible remonstrance against Christmas day, grounded upon divine Scriptures, 2 Cor. v. 16; 1 Cor. xv. 14. 17; and in honour of the Lord's Day, grounded upon these Scriptures, John xx. 1; Rev. i. 10; Psalms, cxviii. 24; Lev. xxiii. 7, 11; Mark xv. 8; Psalms, lxxxiv. 10; in which Christmas is called Anti-christ's masse, and those Masse-mongers and Papists who observe it, &c. In consequence of which Parliament spent some time in consultation about the abolition of Christmas day, passed orders to that effect and resolved to sit on the following day which was commonly called Christmas day."

champions of the Round Heads, on the subject of Christmas festivity; and concluded by urging his hearers, in the most solemn and affecting manner, to stand to the traditional customs of their fathers, and feast and make merry on this joyful anniversary of the church.

I have seldom known a sermon attended apparently with more immediate effects; for on leaving the church, the congregation seemed one and all possessed with the gayety of spirit so earnestly enjoined by their pastor. The elder folks gathered in knots in the churchyard, greeting and shaking hands; and the children ran about crying, "Ule! Ule!" and repeating some uncouth rhymes,* which the parson, who had joined us, informed me, had been handed down from days of yore. The villagers doffed their hats to the 'Squire as he passed, giving him the good wishes of the season with every appearance of heartfelt sincerity, and were invited by him to the hall, to take something to keep out the cold of the weather; and I heard blessings uttered by several of the poor, which convinced me that, in the midst of his enjoyments, the worthy old cavalier had not forgotten the true Christmas virtue of charity.

On our way homeward, his heart seemed overflowing with generous and happy feelings. As we passed over a rising ground which commanded something of a prospect, the sounds of rustic merriment now and then reached our ears; the 'Squire paused for a few moments, and looked around with an air of inexpressible benignity. The beauty of the day was, of itself, sufficient to inspire philanthropy. Notwithstanding the frostiness of the morning, the sun in his cloudless journey had acquired sufficient power to melt away the thin covering of snow from every southern declivity, and to bring out the living green which adorns an English landscape even in mid-winter. Large tracts of smiling verdure contrasted with the dazzling whiteness of the shaded slopes and hollows.

---

* "Ule! Ule!
Three puddings in a pule;
Crack nuts and cry ule!"

Every sheltered bank on which the broad rays rested, yielded its silver rill of cold and limpid water, glittering through the dripping grass ; and sent up slight exhalations to contribute to the thin haze that hung just above the surface of the earth. There was something truly cheering in this triumph of warmth and verdure over the frosty thraldom of winter; it was, as the 'Squire observed, an emblem of Christmas hospitality, breaking through the chills of ceremony and selfishness, and thawing every heart into a flow. He pointed with pleasure to the indications of good cheer reeking from the chimneys of the comfortable farm-houses and low thatched cottages. " I love," said he, " to see this day well kept by rich and poor ; it is a great thing to have one day in the year, at least, when you are sure of being welcome wherever you go, and of having, as it were, the world all thrown open to you ; and I am almost disposed to join with poor Robin, in his malediction on every churlish enemy to this honest festival :

> " ' Those who at Christmas do repine,
> And would fain hence dispatch him,
> May they with old Duke Humphry dine,
> Or else may 'Squire Ketch catch him.' "

The 'Squire went on to lament the deplorable decay of the games and amusements which were once prevalent at this season among the lower orders, and countenanced by the higher; when the old halls of castles and manor-houses were thrown open at daylight ; when the tables were covered with brawn, and beef, and humming ale; when the harp and the carol resounded all day long, and when rich and poor were alike welcome to enter and make merry.* " Our old games and local customs," said he, " had a great effect in making the

---

* "An English gentleman at the opening of the great day, *i.e.* on Christmas day in the morning, had all his tenants and neighbors enter his hall by daybreak. The strong beer was broached, and the black-jacks went plentifully about with toast, sugar, and nutmeg and good Cheshire cheese. The Hackin (the great sausage) must be boiled by daybreak, or else two young men must take the maiden (*i.e.* the cook) by the arms and run her round the market-place till she is shamed of her laziness."—*Round about our Sea-Coal Fire.*

peasant fond of his home, and the promotion of them by the gentry made him fond of his lord. They made the times merrier, and kinder, and better, and I can truly say with one of our old poets,

> "'I like them well—the curious preciseness
> And all-pretended gravity of those
> That seek to banish hence these harmless sports,
> Have thrust away much ancient honesty.'

"The nation," continued he, "is altered; we have almost lost our simple true-hearted peasantry. They have broken asunder from the higher classes, and seem to think their interests are separate. They have become too knowing, and begin to read newspapers, listen to alehouse politicians, and talk of reform. I think one mode to keep them in good humor in these hard times would be for the nobility and gentry to pass more time on their estates, mingle more among the country people, and set the merry old English games going again."

Such was the good 'Squire's project for mitigating public discontent : and, indeed, he had once attempted to put his doctrine in practice, and a few years before had kept open house during the holidays in the old style. The country people, however, did not understand how to play their parts in the scene of hospitality ; many uncouth circumstances occurred; the manor was overrun by all the vagrants of the country, and more beggars drawn into the neighborhood in one week than the parish officers could get rid of in a year. Since then, he had contented himself with inviting the decent part of the neighboring peasantry to call at the Hall on Christmas day, and with distributing beef, and bread, and ale, among the poor, that they might make merry in their own dwellings.

We had not been long home, when the sound of music was heard from a distance. A band of country lads, without coats, their shirt-sleeves fancifully tied with ribbons, their hats decorated with greens, and clubs in their hands, were seen advancing up the avenue, followed by a large number of villagers and peasantry. They stopped before the hall door, where the music struck up a peculiar air, and the lads performed a curious and intricate dance, advancing, retreating, and striking their clubs together, keeping exact time to the music; while one, whimsically crowned with a fox's skin, the tail of which flaunted down his back, kept capering round the skirts of the dance, and rattling a Christmas-box with many antic gesticulations.

The 'Squire eyed this fanciful exhibition with great interest and delight, and gave me a full account of its origin, which he traced to the times when the Romans held possession of the island ; plainly proving that this was a lineal descendant of the sword-dance of the ancients. "It was now," he said, " nearly extinct, but he had accidentally met with traces of it in the neighborhood, and had encouraged its revival ; though, to tell the truth, it was too apt to be followed up by rough cudgel-play, and broken heads, in the evening."

After the dance was concluded, the whole party was entertained with brawn and beef, and stout home-brewed. The 'Squire himself mingled among the rustics, and was received with awkward demonstrations of deference and regard. It is true, I perceived two or three of the younger peasants, as they were raising their tankards to their mouths, when the 'Squire's back was turned, making something of a grimace, and giving each other the wink; but the moment they caught my eye they pulled grave faces, and were exceedingly demure. With Master Simon, however, they all seemed more at their ease. His varied occupations and amusements had made him well known throughout the neighborhood. He was a visitor at every farm-house and cottage; gossiped with the farmers and their wives; romped with their daughters; and, like that type of a vagrant bachelor the humble-bee, tolled the sweets from all the rosy lips of the country round.

The bashfulness of the guests soon gave way before good cheer and affability. There is something genuine and affectionate in the gayety of the lower orders, when it is excited by the bounty and familiarity of those above them; the warm glow of gratitude enters into their mirth, and a kind word or a small pleasantry frankly uttered by a patron gladdens the heart of the dependant more than oil and wine. When the 'Squire had retired, the merriment increased, and there was much joking and laughter, particularly between Master Simon and a hale, ruddy-faced, white-headed farmer, who appeared to be the wit of the village; for I observed all his companions to wait with open mouths for his retorts, and burst into a gratuitous, laugh before they could well understand them.

The whole house indeed seemed abandoned to merriment. As I passed to my room to dress for dinner, I heard the sound of music in a small court, and looking through a window that commanded it, I perceived a band of wandering musicians, with pandean pipes, and tambourine; a pretty coquettish housemaid was dancing a jig with a smart country lad, while several of the other servants were looking on. In the midst of her sport, the girl caught a glimpse of my face at the window, and coloring up, ran off with an air of roguish affected confusion.

THE CHRISTMAS DINNER.

Lo, now is come our joyful'st feast!
  Let every man be jolly,
Each roome with yvie leaves is drest,
  And every post with holly.
    Now all our neighbours' chimneys smoke,
    And Christmas blocks are burning;
    Their ovens they with bak't meats choke,
    And all their spits are turning,
      Without the door let sorrow lie,
      And if, for cold, it hap to die,
      Wee 'l bury 't in a Christmas pye,
      And evermore be merry.

WITHERS, *Juvenilia.*

I HAD finished my toilet, and was loitering with Frank Bracebridge in the library, when he heard a distant thwacking sound, which he informed me was a signal for the serving

up of the dinner.   The 'Squire kept up old customs in kitchen
as well as hall; and the rolling-pin struck upon the dresser
by the cook, summoned the servants to carry in the meats.

> Just in this nick the cook knock'd thrice,
> And all the waiters in a trice,
>   His summons did obey;
> Each serving man, with dish in hand,
> Marched boldly up, like our train band,
>   Presented, and away.*

The dinner was served up in the great hall, where the
'Squire always held his Christmas banquet.   A blazing crack-
ling fire of logs had been heaped on to warm the spacious
apartment, and the flame went sparkling and wreathing up
the wide-mouthed chimney.   The great picture of the crusader and his white horse had been profusely decorated with
greens for the occasion ; and holly and ivy had likewise been
wreathed round the helmet and weapons on the opposite wall,
which I understood were the arms of the same warrior.   I
must own, by the bye, I had strong doubts about the authen-
ticity of the painting and armor as having belonged to the
crusader, they certainly having the stamp of more recent
days ; but I was told that the painting had been so considered
time out of mind ; and that, as to the armor, it had been
found in a lumber-room, and elevated to its present situation
by the 'Squire, who at once determined it to be the armor
of the family hero ; and as he was absolute authority on all
such subjects in his own household, the matter had passed
into current acceptation.   A sideboard was set out just under
this chivalric trophy, on which was a display of plate that
might have vied (at least in variety) with Belshazzar's parade
of the vessels of the temple ; "flagons, cans, cups, beakers,
goblets, basins, and ewers ;" the gorgeous utensils of good
companionship that had gradually accumulated through many
generations of jovial housekeepers.   Before these stood the
two yule candles, beaming like two stars of the first magnitude ; other lights were distributed in branches, and the whole
array glittered like a firmament of silver.

----

* Sir John Suckling.

We were ushered into this banqueting scene with the sound of minstrelsy; the old harper being seated on a stool beside the fire-place, and tr.anging his instrument with a vast deal more power than melody. Never did Christmas board display a more goodly and gracious assemblage of countenances; those who were not handsome, were, at least, happy; and happiness is a rare improver of your hard-favored visage. I always consider an old English family as well worth studying as a collection of Holbein's portraits, or Albert Durer's prints. There is much antiquarian lore to be acquired; much knowledge of the physiognomies of former times. Perhaps it may be from having continually before their eyes those rows of old family portraits, with which the mansions of this country are stocked; certain it is, that the quaint features of antiquity are often most faithfully perpetuated in these ancient lines; and I have traced an old family nose through a whole picture gallery, legitimately handed down from generation to generation, almost from the time of the Conquest. Something of the kind was to be observed in the worthy company around me. Many of their faces had evidently originated in a Gothic age, and been merely copied by succeeding generations; and there was one little girl, in particular, of staid demeanor, with a high Roman nose, and an antique vinegar aspect, who was a great favorite of the 'Squire's, being, as he said, a Bracebridge all over, and the very counterpart of one of his ancestors who figured in the Court of Henry VIII.

The parson said grace, which was not a short familiar one, such as is commonly addressed to the Deity in these unceremonious days; but a long, courtly, well-worded one of the ancient school. There was now a pause, as if something was expected; when suddenly the butler entered the hall with some degree of bustle; he was attended by a servant on each side with a large wax-light, and bore a silver dish, on which was an enormous pig's head, decorated with rosemary, with a lemon in its mouth, which was placed with great formality at the head of the table. The moment this

pageant made its appearance, the harper struck up a flourish ;
at the conclusion of which the young Oxonian, on receiving
a nod from the 'Squire, gave, with an air of the most comic
gravity an old carol, the first verse of which was as follows :

> Caput apri defero
> Reddens laudes Domino.
> The boar's head in hand bring I,
> With garland's gay and rosemary.
> I pray you all synge merily
> Qui estis in convivio.

Though prepared to witness many of these little eccentricities, from being apprised of the peculiar hobby of mine
host ; yet, I confess, the parade with which so odd a dish
was introduced somewhat perplexed me, until I gathered
from the conversation of the 'Squire and the parson, that it
was meant to represent the bringing in of the boar's head—a
dish formerly served up with much ceremony, and the sound
of minstrelsy and song, at great tables on Christmas day. "I
like the old custom," said the 'Squire, "not merely because
it is stately and pleasing in itself, but because it was observed
at the college at Oxford, at which I was educated.   When I
hear the old song chanted, it brings to mind the time when
I was young and gamesome—and the noble old college hall—
and my fellow-students loitering about in their black gowns ;
many of whom, poor lads, are now in their graves ! "

The parson, however, whose mind was not haunted by
such associations, and who was always more taken up with
the text than the sentiment, objected to the Oxonian's version
of the carol ; which he affirmed was different from that sung
at college.   He went on, with the dry perseverance of a com-
mentator, to give the college reading, accompanied by sundry
annotations ; addressing himself at first to the company at
large ; but finding their attention gradually diverted to other
talk, and other objects, he lowered his tone as his number of
auditors diminished, until he concluded his remarks in an
under voice, to a fat-headed old gentleman next him, who

was silently engaged in the discussion of a huge plateful of turkey.*

The table was literally loaded with good cheer, and presented an epitome of country abundance, in this season of overflowing larders. A distinguished post was allotted to "ancient sirloin," as mine host termed it ; being, as he added, "the standard of old English hospitality, and a joint of goodly presence, and full of expectation." There were several dishes quaintly decorated, and which had evidently something traditional in their embellishments ; but about which, as I did not like to appear over-curious, I asked no questions.

I could not, however, but notice a pie, magnificently decorated with peacocks' feathers, in imitation of the tail of that bird, which overshadowed a considerable tract of the table. This, the 'Squire confessed, with some little hesitation, was a pheasant pie, though a peacock pie was certainly the most authentical ; but there had been such a mortality among

---

* The old ceremony of serving up the boar's head on Christmas day, is still observed in the hall of Queen's College, Oxford. I was favored by the parson with a copy of the carol as now sung, and as it may be acceptable to such of my readers as are curious in these grave and learned matters, I give it entire:

> The boar's head in hand bear I,
> Bedeck'd with bays and rosemary ;
> And I pray you, my masters, be merry,
>   Quot estis in convivio,
>   Caput apri defero.
>   Reddens laudes Domino.
>
> The boar's head as I understand,
> Is the rarest dish in all this land,
> Which thus bedeck'd with a gay garland
>   Let us servire cantico.
>   Caput apri defero, etc.
>
> Our steward hath provided this
> In honor of the King of Bliss,
> Which on this day to be served is
>   In Riginensi Atrio.
>   Caput apri defero.
>   Etc., etc., etc.

the peacocks this season, that he could not prevail upon himself to have one killed.*

It would be tedious, perhaps, to my wiser readers, who may not have that foolish fondness for odd and obsolete things to which I am a little given, were I to mention the other makeshifts of this worthy old humorist, by which he was endeavoring to follow up, though at humble distance, the quaint customs of antiquity. I was pleased, however, to see the respect shown to his whims by his children and relatives ; who, indeed, entered readily into the full spirit of them, and seemed all well versed in their parts ; having doubtless been present at many a rehearsal. I was amused, too, at the air of profound gravity with which the butler and other servants executed the duties assigned them, however eccentric. They had an old-fashioned look ; having for the most part, been brought up in the household, and grown into keeping with the antiquated mansion, and the humors of its lord ; and most probably looked upon all his whimsical regulations as the established laws of honorable housekeeping.

When the cloth was removed, the butler brought in a huge silver vessel, of rare and curious workmanship, which he placed before the 'Squire. Its appearance was hailed with acclamation ; being the Wassail Bowl, so renowned in Christmas festivity. The contents had been prepared by the 'Squire himself ; for it was a beverage, in the skilful mixture of

---

* The peacock was anciently in great demand for stately entertainments. Sometimes it was made into a pie, at one end of which the head appeared above the crust in all its plumage, with the beak richly gilt ; at the other end the tail was displayed. Such pies were served up at the solemn banquets of chivalry, when Knights errant pledged themselves to undertake any perilous enterprise, whence came the ancient oath, used by Justice Shallow, "by cock and pie."

The peacock was also an important dish for the Christmas feast; and Massinger, in his City Madam, gives some idea of the extravagance with which this, as well as other dishes, was prepared for the gorgeous revels of the olden times:

Men may talk of Country Christmases.

Their thirty pound butter'd eggs, their pies of carps' tongues:

Their pheasants drench'd with ambergris; *the carcases of three fat wethers bruised for gravy to make sauce for a single peacock!*

which he particularly prided himself ; alleging that it was too abstruse and complex for the comprehension of an ordinary servant. It was a potation, indeed, that might well make the heart of a toper leap within him ; being composed of the richest and raciest wines, highly spiced and sweetened, with roasted apples bobbing about the surface.*

The old gentleman's whole countenance beamed with a serene look of indwelling delight, as he stirred this mighty bowl. Having raised it to his lips, with a hearty wish of a merry Christmas to all present, he sent it brimming round the board, for every one to follow his example according to the primitive style ; pronouncing it " the ancient fountain of good feeling, where all hearts met together." †

There was much laughing and rallying, as the honest emblem of Christmas joviality circulated, and was kissed rather coyly by the ladies. But when it reached Master Simon, he raised it in both hands, and with the air of a boon companion, struck up an old Wassail Chanson :

> The brown bowle,
> The merry brown bowle,
> As it goes round aboute-a,
>   Fill
>   Still,
> Let the world say what it will,
> And drink your fill all out-a.

---

* The Wassail Bowl was sometimes composed of ale instead of wine; with nutmeg, sugar, toast, ginger, and roasted crabs; in this way the nut-brown beverage is still prepared in some old families, and round the hearth of substantial farmers at Christmas. It is also called Lamb's Wool, and it is celebrated by Herrick in his Twelfth Night:

> Next crowne the bowle full
> With gentle Lamb's Wool,
> Add sugar, nutmeg, and ginger,
> With store of ale too,
> And thus ye must doe
> To make the Wassaile a swinger.

† " The custom of drinking out of the same cup gave place to each having his cup. When the steward came to the doore with the Wassel, he was to cry three times, *Wassel, Wassel, Wassel,* and then the chappell (chaplain) was to answer with a song."—*Archæologia.*

The deep canne,
The merry deep canne,
As thou dost freely quaff-a,
    Sing
    Fling,
Be as merry as a king,
And sound a lusty laugh-a.*

Much of the conversation during dinner turned upon
family topics, to which I was a stranger. There was, however, a great deal of rallying of Master Simon about some gay
widow, with whom he was accused of having a flirtation.
This attack was commenced by the ladies; but it was continued throughout the dinner by the fat-headed old gentleman next the parson, with the persevering assiduity of a slow
hound; being one of these long-winded jokers, who, though
rather dull at starting game, are unrivalled for their talents
in hunting it down.   At every pause in the general conversation, he renewed his bantering in pretty much the same
terms; winking hard at me with both eyes, whenever he gave
Master Simon what he considered a home thrust.   The latter,
indeed, seemed fond of being teased on the subject, as old
bachelors are apt to be; and he took occasion to inform me,
in an undertone, that the lady in question was a prodigiously
fine woman and drove her own curricle.

The dinner-time passed away in this flow of innocent
hilarity, and though the old hall may have resounded in its
time with many a scene of broader rout and revel, yet I doubt
whether it ever witnessed more honest and genuine enjoyment.
How easy it is for one benevolent being to diffuse pleasure
around him; and how truly is a kind heart a fountain of
gladness, making everything in its vicinity to freshen into
smiles!   The joyous disposition of the worthy 'Squire was
perfectly contagious; he was happy himself, and disposed to
make all the world happy; and the little eccentricities of his
humor did but season, in a manner, the sweetness of his
philanthropy.

---

* From Poor Robin's Almanack.

When the ladies had retired, the conversation, as usual, became still more animated.

The 'Squire told several long stories of early college pranks and adventures, in some of which the parson had been a sharer; though in looking at the latter, it required some effort of imagination to figure such a little dark anatomy of a man, into the perpetrator of a madcap gambol. Indeed, the two college chums presented pictures of what men may be made by their different lots in life: the 'Squire had left the university to live lustily on his paternal domains, in the vigorous enjoyment of prosperity and sunshine, and had flourished on to a hearty and florid old age; whilst the poor parson, on the contrary, had dried and withered away, among dusty tomes, in the silence and shadows of his study. Still there seemed to be a spark of almost extinguished fire, feebly glimmering in the bottom of his soul; and, as the 'Squire hinted at a sly story of the parson and a pretty milkmaid whom they once met on the banks of the Isis, the old gentleman made an "alphabet of faces," which, as far as I could deciper his physiognomy, I verily believe was indicative of laughter,—indeed, I have rarely met with an old gentleman that took absolute offence at the imputed gallantries of his youth.

After the dinner-table was removed, the hall was given up to the younger members of the family, who, prompted to all kind of noisy mirth by the Oxonian and Master Simon, made its old walls ring with their merriment, as they played at romping games. I delight in witnessing the gambols of children, and particularly at this happy holiday season, and could not help stealing out of the drawing-room on hearing one of their peals of laughter. I found them at the game of blind-man's-buff. Master Simon, who was the leader of their revels, and seemed on all occasions to fulfil the office of that ancient potentate, the Lord of Misrule,* was blinded in the

* At Christmas there was in the Kinges house, wheresoever hee was lodged, a lorde of misrule, or mayster of merie disportes, and the like lad ye in the house of every nobleman of honor; or good worshippe, were he spirituall or temporall.—STOW.

midst of the hall. The little beings were as busy about him as the mock fairies about Falstaff; pinching him, plucking at the skirts of his coat, and tickling him with straws. One fine blue-eyed girl of about thirteen, with her flaxen hair all in beautiful confusion, her frolic face in a glow, her frock half torn off her shoulders, a complete picture of a romp, was the chief tormentor; and from the slyness with which Master Simon avoided the smaller game, and hemmed this wild little nymph in corners, and obliged her to jump shrieking over chairs, I suspected the rogue of being not a whit more blinded than was convenient.

When I returned to the drawing-room, I found the company seated round the fire, listening to the parson, who was deeply ensconced in a high-backed oaken chair, the work of some cunning artificer of yore, which had been brought from the library for his particular accommodation. From this venerable piece of furniture, with which his shadowy figure and dark weazen face so admirably accorded, he was dealing forth strange accounts of the popular superstitions and legends of the surrounding country, with which he had become acquainted in the course of his antiquarian researches. I am inclined to think that the old gentleman was himself somewhat tinctured with superstition, as men are very apt to be, who live a recluse and studious life in a sequestered part of the country, and pour over black-letter tracts, so often filled with the marvellous and supernatural. He gave us several anecdotes of the fancies of the neighboring peasantry, concerning the effigy of the crusader, which lay on the tomb by the church altar. As it was the only monument of the kind in that part of the country, it had always been regarded with feelings of superstition by the good wives of the village. It was said to get up from the tomb and walk the rounds of the churchyard in stormy nights, particularly when it thundered; and one old woman whose cottage bordered on the churchyard, had seen it through the windows of the church, when the moon shone, slowly pacing up and down the aisles. It was the belief that some wrong had been left unredressed by the deceased, or some treasure hidden, which kept the spirit in a state of trouble and restlessness. Some talked of gold and jewels buried in the tomb, over which the spectre kept watch ; and there was a story current of a sexton, in old times, who endeavored to break his way to the coffin at night ; but just as he reached it received a violent blow from the marble hand of the effigy, which stretched him senseless on the pavement. These tales were often laughed at by some of the sturdier among the rustics ; yet, when night came on, there were many of the stoutest unbelievers that were shy of venturing alone in the footpath that led across the churchyard.

From these and other anecdotes that followed, the crusader appeared to be the favorite hero of ghost stories throughout the vicinity. His picture, which hung up in the hall, was thought by the servants to have something supernatural about it : for they remarked that, in whatever part of the hall you went, the eyes of the warrior were still fixed on you. The old porter's wife, too, at the lodge, who had been born and brought up in the family, and was a great gossip among the maid-servants, affirmed, that in her young days she had often heard say, that on Midsummer eve, when it was well known all kinds of ghosts, goblins, and fairies, become visible and walk abroad, the crusader used to mount his horse, come down from his picture, ride about the house, down the avenue, and so to the church to visit the tomb ; on which occasion the church door most civilly swung open of itself ; not that he needed it—for he rode through closed gates and even stone walls, and had been seen by one of the dairy-maids to pass between two bars of the great park gate, making himself as thin as a sheet of paper.

All these superstitions I found had been very much countenanced by the Squire, who though not superstitious himself, was very fond of seeing others so. He listened to every goblin tale of the neighboring gossips with infinite gravity, and held the porter's wife in high favor on account of her talent for the marvelous. He was himself a great reader of old legends and romances, and often lamented that he could not believe in them; for a superstitious person, he thought, must live in a kind of fairy land.

Whilst we were all attention to the parson's stories, our ears were suddenly assailed by a burst of heterogeneous sounds from the hall, in which were mingled something like the clang of rude minstrelsy, with the uproar of many small voices and girlish laughter. The door suddenly flew open, and a train came trooping into the room, that might almost have been mistaken for the breaking up of the court of Fairy. That indefatigable spirit, Master Simon, in the faithful discharge of his duties as lord of misrule, had conceived the idea of a Christmas mummery, or masking; and having called in to his assistance the Oxonian and the young officer, who were equally ripe for anything that should occasion romping and merriment, they had carried it into instant effect. The old housekeeper had been consulted; the antique clothes-presses and wardrobes rummaged, and made to yield up the relics of finery that had not seen the light for several generations : the younger part of the company had been privately convened from parlor and hall, and the whole had been bedizened out, into a burlesque imitation of an antique masque.*

Master Simon led the van as "Ancient Christmas," quaintly apparelled in a ruff, short cloak, which had very much the aspect of one of the old housekeeper's petticoats, and a hat that might have served for a village steeple and must indubitably have figured in the days of the Covenanters. From under this, his nose curved boldly forth, flushed with a frost-bitten bloom that seemed the very trophy of a December blast. He was accompanied by the blue-eyed romp, dished up as "Dame Mince Pie," in the venerable magnificence of faded brocade, long stomacher, peaked hat and high-heeled shoes.

The young officer appeared as Robin Hood, in a sporting dress of Kendal green, and a foraging cap with a gold tassel.

---

* Maskings or mummeries were favorite sports at Christmas, in old times, and the wardrobes at halls and manor-houses were often laid under contribution to furnish dresses and fantastic disguisings. I strongly suspect Master Simon to have taken the idea of his from Ben Jonson's Mask of Christmas.

The costume, to be sure, did not bear testimony to deep research, and there was an evident eye to the picturesque natural to a young gallant in presence of his mistress. The fair Julia hung on his arm in a pretty rustic dress, as "Maid Marian." The rest of the train had been metamorphosed in various ways; the girls trussed up in the finery of the ancient belles of the Bracebridge line, and the striplings bewhiskered with burnt cork, and gravely clad in broad skirts, hanging sleeves, and full-bottomed wigs, to represent the characters of Roast Beef, Plum Pudding, and other worthies celebrated in ancient maskings. The whole was under the control of the Oxonian, in the appropriate character of Misrule; and I observed that he exercised rather a mischievous sway with his wand over the smaller personages of the pageant.

The irruption of this motley crew, with beat of drum, according to ancient custom, was the consummation of uproar and merriment. Master Simon covered himself with glory by the stateliness with which, as Ancient Christmas, he walked a minuet with the peerless, though giggling, Dame Mince Pie. It was followed by a dance from all the characters, which, from its medley of costumes, seemed as though the old family portraits had skipped down from their frames to join in the sport. Different centuries were figuring at cross-hands and right and left; the Dark Ages were cutting pirouettes and rigadoons; and the days of Queen Bess, jigging merrily down the middle, through a line of succeeding generations.

The worthy 'Squire contemplated these fantastic sports, and this resurrection of his old wardrobe, with the simple relish of childish delight. He stood chuckling and rubbing his hands, and scarcely hearing a word the parson said, notwithstanding that the latter was discoursing most authentically on the ancient and stately dance of the Pavon, or peacock, from which he conceived the minuet to be derived.* For my

---

* Sir John Hawkins, speaking of the dance called the Pavon, from pavo, a peacock, says. "It is a grave and majestic dance: the method of dancing it anciently was by gentlemen dressed with caps and swords, by those of the long robe in their gowns; by the peers in their mantles, and by the ladies in gowns with long trains, the motion whereof, in dancing, resembled that of a peacock.—*History of Music.*

part, I was in a continual excitement from the varied scenes of whim and innocent gayety passing before me. It was inspiring to see wild-eyed frolic and warm-hearted hospitality breaking out from among the chills and glooms of winter, and old age throwing off his apathy, and catching once more the freshness of youthful enjoyment. I felt also an interest in the scene, from the consideration that these fleeting customs were posting fast into oblivion, and that this was perhaps, the only family in England in which the whole of them were still punctilliously observed. There was a quaintness, too, mingled with all this revelry, that gave it a peculiar zest : it was suited to the time and place ; and as the old Manor-house almost reeled with mirth and wassail, it seemed echoing back the joviality of long-departed years.

———

But enough of Christmas and its gambols ; it is time for me to pause in this garrulity. Methinks I hear the question asked by my graver readers, "To what purpose is all this—how is the world to be made wiser by this talk ?" Alas ! is there not wisdom enough extant for the instruction of the world ? And if not, are there not thousands of abler pens laboring for its improvement ?—It is so much pleasanter to please than to instruct—to play the companion rather than the preceptor.

What, after all, is the mite of wisdom that I could throw into the mass of knowledge ; or how am I sure that my sagest deductions may be safe guides for the opinions of others ? But in writing to amuse, if I fail, the only evil is my own disappointment. If, however, I can by any lucky chance, in these days of evil, rub out one wrinkle from the brow of care, or beguile the heavy heart of one moment of sorrow—if I can now and then penetrate through the gathering film of misanthropy, prompt a benevolent view of human nature, and make my reader more in good humor with his fellow beings and himself, surely, surely, I shall not then have written entirely in vain.

ENGLISH CLASSIC SERIES,

FOR

Classes in English Literature, Reading, Grammar, etc.

EDITED BY EMINENT ENGLISH AND AMERICAN SCHOLARS.

Each Volume contains a Sketch of the Author's Life, Prefatory and Explanatory Notes, etc., etc.

(*Additional numbers on next page.*)

ENGLISH CLASSIC SERIES—CONTINUED.

63 **The Antigone of Sophocles.** English Version by Thos. Francklin, D.D.

64 **Elizabeth Barrett Browning.** (Selected Poems.)

85 **Robert Browning.** (Selected Poems.)

66 **Addison, The Spectator.** (Sel'ns.)

67 **Scenes from George Eliot's Adam Bede.**

68 **Matthew Arnold's Culture and Anarchy.**

69 **DeQuincey's Joan of Arc.**

70 **Carlyle's Essay on Burns.**

71 **Byron's Childe Harold's Pilgrimage.**

72 **Poe's Raven, and other Poems.**

73 & 74 **Macaulay's Lord Clive.** (Double Number.)

75 **Webster's Reply to Hayne.**

76 & 77 **Macaulay's Lays of A cient Rome.** (Double Numbe

78 **American Patriotic Selection** Declaration of Independenc Washington's Farewell A dress, Lincoln's Gettysbu Speech, etc.

79 & 80 **Scott's Lady of the Lak** (Condensed.)

81 & 82 **Scott's Marmion.** (Co densed.)

83 & 84 **Pope's Essay on Man.**

85 **Shelley's Skylark, Adonais, ar** other Poems.

86 **Dickens's Cricket on th** Hearth.

87 **Spencer's Philosophy of Style**

88 **Lamb's Essays of Elia.**

89 **Cowper's Task, Book II.**

90 **Wordsworth's Selected Poem**

Single numbers, 32 to 64 pp. Mailing price, 12 cents per copy.
Double numbers, 75 to 128 pp. Mailing price, 24 cents per copy.

SPECIAL PRICES TO TEACHERS.

SPECIAL NUMBERS.

Milton's Paradise Lost. Book I. With portrait and bi graphical sketch of Milton, essay on his genius, epitome of the views of the bes known critics, Milton's verse, argument, and full introductory and explanator notes. Bound in boards. *Mailing price, 30 cents.*

Milton's Paradise Lost. Books I. and II. With portrait an biographical sketch of Milton, his verse; essay on his genius, epitome of the view of the best-known critics, argument, and full introductory and axplanatory note Bound in boards. *Mailing price, 40 cents.*

Wykes's Shakespeare Reader. Being extracts from th Plays of Shakespeare, with introductory paragraphs, and grammatical, historica and explanatory notes. By C. H. WYKES. 160 pp., 16mo, cloth. *Mailing pric 35 cents.*

Chaucer's The Canterbury Tales. The Prologue. Th text collated with the seven oldest MSS., a portrait and biographical sketch of the author, introductory notices, grammar, critical and explanatory notes, index to obsolete and difficult words, argument and characters of the prologue, brief histor of English language to time of Chaucer, and glossary. Bound in boards. *Mailin price, 35 cents.*

Chaucer's The Squieres Tale. With portrait and biograph ica. sketch of author, introduction to his grammar and versification, glossary, ex amination papers, and full explanatory notes. Bound iu boards. *Mailing price 35 cents.*

Chaucer's The Knightes Tale. With portrait and bio graphical sketch of author, essay on his language, history of the English language to time of Chaucer, glossary, and full explanatory notes. Bound in beards. *Mail ing price, 40 cents.*

Goldsmith's She Stoops to Conquer. With biographical sketch of author, introduction, dedication, Garrick's Prologue, epilogue and three intended epilogues, and full explanatory notes. Bound in boards. *Mailing price, 30 cents.*

FULL DESCRIPTIVE CATALOGUE SENT ON APPLICATION.